"Would You Please Get Out Of Here?"

Kit said. She'd never been alone in this kind of intimate setting with Logan.

He made an odd, hesitant movement and sat down on the bed beside her. His big hand folded around both of hers and detached them from their death grip on the coverlet. "What are you afraid of?" he asked.

He'd never used that tone with her—his voice had a deep, husky pitch that was like warm velvet. She looked into his eyes, closer than she'd ever seen them, and became lost in their dark brown depths.

"Answer me, Kit."

"I'm not afraid of you," she said.

"I won't hurt you," he whispered, moving even closer. "I can be gentle...."

Dear Reader,

I know you can't wait to get your hands on September's Silhouette Desire books! First, because September has the latest installment in Diana Palmer's MOST WANTED series—*The Case of the Missing Secretary.* And don't worry if you missed earlier books in the series; each story stands on its own.

Next, because September has Annette Broadrick, and the start of her new series, the SONS OF TEXAS. This month we have *Love Texas Style!* Look for *Courtship Texas Style!* in October and *Marriage Texas Style!* in November.

And, of course, there's this month's thrilling, sexy, wonderful *Man of the Month, Navarrone,* by Helen R. Myers. And September is completed with fabulous stories by Laura Leone, Jean Barrett and a talented newcomer I know you'll love, Mary Maxwell.

Don't miss any of these. I couldn't begin to pick a favorite—they're all so terrific—and I'll bet you couldn't, either.

All the best,

Lucia Macro
Senior Editor

DIANA PALMER
THE CASE OF THE
MISSING SECRETARY

SILHOUETTE *Desire*®
Published by Silhouette Books New York
America's Publisher of Contemporary Romance

SILHOUETTE BOOKS
300 East 42nd St., New York, N.Y. 10017

THE CASE OF THE MISSING SECRETARY

ISBN: 0-373-05733-4

First Silhouette Books printing September 1992

Printed in the U.S.A.

Books by Diana Palmer

Silhouette Desire

The Cowboy and the Lady #12
September Morning #26
Friends and Lovers #50
Fire and Ice #80
Snow Kisses #102
Diamond Girl #110
The Rawhide Man #157
Lady Love #175
Cattleman's Choice #193
The Tender Stranger #230
Love by Proxy #252
Eye of the Tiger #271
Loveplay #289
Rawhide and Lace #306
Rage of Passion #325
Fit for a King #349
Betrayed by Love #391
Enamored #420
Reluctant Father #469
Hoodwinked #492
His Girl Friday #528
Hunter #606
Nelson's Brand #618
The Best Is Yet To Come #643
‡*The Case of the Mesmerizing Boss* #702
‡*The Case of the Confirmed Bachelor* #715
‡*The Case of the Missing Secretary* #733

Silhouette Special Edition

Heather's Song #33
The Australian #239

Silhouette Romance

Darling Enemy #254
Roomful of Roses #301
Heart of Ice #314
Passion Flower #328
Soldier of Fortune #340
After the Music #406
Champagne Girl #436
Unlikely Lover #472
Woman Hater #532
*Calhoun #580
*Justin #592
*Tyler #604
*Sutton's Way #670
*Ethan #694
*Connal #741
*Harden #783
*Evan #819
*Donavan #843

Silhouette Books

Silhouette Christmas Stories 1987
''The Humbug Man''
Silhouette Summer Sizzlers 1990
''Miss Greenhorn''

Also by Diana Palmer

Diana Palmer Duets Books I-VI
Diana Palmer Collection

*Long, Tall Texans
‡Most Wanted Series

With love to SPC Tracy Adams 4th MMC,
13th COSCOM—please write!

One

Kit Morris was just barely lucid as she stormed into the Lassiter Detective Agency, her short black hair falling in wet strings around her face, her blue eyes huge and red-rimmed. Her tall, slender figure was clad in a gray suit that had been immaculate just that morning, paired with a soft white blouse and an extravagant silk blue-patterned scarf. Now, the whole outfit was a dripping mess—like Kit's nerves.

It was Tess Lassiter's day substituting for her husband Dane's receptionist, so she was the first person Kit saw when she dragged into the office. Kit and Tess had been best friends for years, long before Tess married Dane Lassiter, who'd been Tess's boss at the time. Kit and Tess had a lot in common. Not that Kit had a single bald chance of ever marrying *her* boss. Her *ex*-boss, that was. At the moment, Kit would much rather stand him up against a mesquite tree and put a fountain pen through his black heart than walk down the aisle with him.

"What happened to you?" Tess exclaimed. "My goodness, Kit, you look terrible!"

"Of course I look terrible! He put me out of the car on Travis Street!"

"That's five blocks from here," Tess mumbled. "He who?"

"Can't you guess?" Kit wailed. "It was *him!* My boss! My ex-boss," she corrected furiously, shaking her head to get the hair out of her eyes. "He...he hijacked me from the public safety department where I was getting my driver's license renewed!" she exclaimed.

"He *hijacked* you?" Tess had to smother a laugh.

"Yes! I didn't want to go with him, but he picked me up and carried me out to the car. And in front of all those people," she groaned. "I didn't even get my license fee paid! I'll have to go back again and stand in line for another hour!"

"Oh, Kit," Tess began sympathetically.

"I resigned two weeks ago, after all! I don't work for him anymore! He can't talk to me like that!"

"Like what?" Tess asked soothingly, trying to calm her best friend.

Kit's eyes blazed like blue flames. "All these years I've slaved for him." She choked. "Taking his dictation, following him around the world, withstanding his disgusting temper...and he has the gall...the *gall* to say that I'm not worth the salary he used to pay me!

As if it was a king's ransom or something. Can you imagine?"

"Mr. Deverell said that?"

"Logan Deverell is a tyrant and a beast." Kit fumed. "The lowest of the low. A worm! No." She caught herself. "Pond scum! That's what he is, only much, much lower...."

"Did you do something?" Tess probed gently.

"Not since I told him about his new conquest, right before I quit," she muttered, trying to hide her feeling of heartbreak. Logan Deverell's new woman was why Kit had quit her job in the first place. "He's serious about her, you know."

"But why did he nab you?"

Kit threw up her graceful hands. "Who knows? Anyway, he tried to coax me into coming back and I told him I wouldn't. He practically jumped down my throat with both feet. He's never used language like that to me, and he said that I was worthless as a secretary and he didn't know why he was willing to hire me again."

Tess wanted to get up and put her arms around the taller woman and coax her to cry. But Kit was stubborn, even in grief. She held her chin high, struggling to maintain her dignity. Tess couldn't undermine her strength.

She could only imagine how her friend was hurting. Kit had been in love with Logan Deverell for years. The silly man never noticed her, except as a piece of office furniture.

"Why was he offering you your old job back?" Tess asked.

"I don't know. We started arguing before he got around to telling me. He was raging like a madman. I didn't even think, I just got out of the car and left."

"He put you out in the rain?" Tess groaned. "How could he!"

"He didn't put me out as much as I jumped out," Kit confessed. "The stupid blind man! I love him so!" Kit choked. Her heart felt as if it were something brittle that had just been smacked with a bat. She was coming unglued. "If only I were blond and stacked!"

"Who is this woman he's seeing?" Tess asked.

"Betsy Corley," she said huskily.

"I don't know her."

"I do. At least, I know *of* her. At one time I was good friends with the man in my apartment building that she took for everything he had." Kit took a steadying breath. "Logan is determined to marry her," she said and laughed hoarsely.

"Oh, Kit," Tess groaned sympathetically.

"At least I have a job, thanks to you and Dane," she said miserably. "I've burned all my bridges...."

"Well, in that case, it's a good thing we're making a detective out of you," Dane Lassiter murmured dryly. He joined the two women, slipping an arm around his wife. He smiled at her before his dark eyes went back to Kit. "We're glad to have you now that Helen's gone to South America where Harold's next job is. He's in the construction business with his father, you remember. And Helen's brother, Nick, is moving back to Washington so that his new wife can keep her tenure at Thorn College. He's starting up his own agency. I'll be two operatives short. That means

I've still got to hire another agent. I'm glad you haven't been tempted to go back to your old boss.''

"I'd be more tempted to step into a lion's mouth than I would to work for Logan Deverell again,'' Kit murmured dryly, hiding her pain. "I hope you know how much I appreciate your giving me a chance here.'' She pushed back her hair again and brushed at the moisture on her suit. It wasn't as wet as she'd first thought, and seemed to be drying slowly.

"We both do,'' Dane told her, smiling. "But you've been quite a surprise, you know. If there are such things as natural born detectives, then I think you're one of them. You've taken to the job like a duck takes to swimming.''

She brightened. "You really think so?''

"I do.''

Kit managed a smile. "Actually I always used to think I'd make a good detective, because I love poking my nose into things that don't concern me.'' She sighed. "You really did save my life by hiring me,'' she persisted. "I didn't have my rent payment. After I stormed out of the office the day I quit, I can't expect Mr. Deverell to send my severance pay after me. I didn't even work a week's notice.''

"I hardly think Logan Deverell will do you out of your severance pay, regardless,'' Dane murmured dryly. "He's not a vindictive man.''

"If you'd seen him ten minutes ago...'' Kit muttered.

Dane cocked an eyebrow as he peered past her. "On second thought,'' he mused, "perhaps he is—''

Before he got the words out, the door flew open and a tall, big dark man in a gray raincoat stormed in.

"I've searched the whole damned city for you," he grumbled, his deep voice like muted thunder in the office as he glared at Kit. "You little fool, you could have been killed, jumping out of a car in the middle of traffic like that! Where in hell have you been?"

"Don't you shout at me!" Kit raged back. "You told me to get my nose out of your business, and I did," she said with painful satisfaction at the grimace on his broad face. "You can find someone else to yell at in your office. Dane says I'm a very good detective!"

Logan Deverell lifted a bushy eyebrow and glanced at Dane. "Did you say that?"

"I'm afraid so," Dane replied. "Under the circumstances, it might be to your advantage not to argue with Kit anymore."

Logan glanced at Kit's face and his lips thinned. He was inclined to agree. She looked shaken. That, and totally out of control emotionally. In all the years she'd worked for him, this was the first time he'd seen her in such a state. She was usually calm and efficient. Except for the day she'd quit, of course, when she'd set new records for abusive verbosity. When he'd followed her into her office, where she was cleaning out her desk, she'd actually thrown a book at him and accused him of mixing her up emotionally with her computer.

It had been the cutting remarks about Betsy being mercenary that had cost Logan his temper today. He still regretted some of the things he'd said. Good secretaries weren't a dime a dozen. He hadn't been able to replace Kit. He missed her madly, though it would be unwise to tell her that, of course. He'd hoped to talk her into coming back, and then she'd mentioned some gossip about Betsy. No way was he going to let *any* woman tell him what to do in his personal life!

"I won't take back what I said," Logan told her. "You had no business meddling in my private life. But I'll apologize for letting you walk back in the rain."

"There's no need to apologize," Kit returned. "It was my fault for ever getting into a car with you in the first place!"

He looked surprised. "I was only going to ask you to come back to work."

"I don't want to come back to work for you, Mr. Deverell," she said icily. "Here, at least, I'm not part of the office furniture. I'm a real live, breathing person with talent and ability, and if I died, Dane and Tess would miss me."

"We've worked together for three years," he reminded her.

"Three years too long," she said, regaining her lost dignity slowly. "I'm sure you'll have no trouble replacing me."

"None of the temporaries can spell," he said angrily. "They can't file, or project a pleasant personality over the phone. Only one of them has any sense at all, and my mother hired her before I knew it. My brother hates the latest addition to the office. She actually told him to get his own coffee!"

"Your brother should have been getting his own coffee for years," she reminded him.

"And my mother's lost again," he added irritably, glancing at Dane. "You'll have to track her down. She told my brother something about a trip to Venice."

"No problem," Dane said. "Just give me her last known location." He studied Kit. "I might let Kit have this assignment. She knows Tansy."

"My mother missed you, too," Logan told Kit with an angry frown. "That's probably why she vanished."

"Go ahead, blame it on me," Kit invited with a sweep of her hand. "I cause your car not to start on cold mornings, I make your coffeepot stop working, I put dust on the windows and make the chairs in the office creak. I probably cause pond scum, too!"

"Will you stop it," Logan muttered. He jammed his big hands into his pockets. Looking at her disturbed him. That was new, and it made him irritable. "Never mind, if you don't want to come back. I can manage without you. Eventually the temporary agency will find me one secretary who can spell, type and answer the telephone."

"Surely they already have?" she asked sarcastically.

"Of course. I just said so, didn't I? The agency found me two more to go with the one that my mother hired. At least she can type. Of the two new ones, only one can spell. The tallest of the three can answer the telephone but it takes her until the fifth ring to find it."

Kit's eyebrows went up. "Why?"

"The desk is buried in unanswered letters and misplaced files," he said simply. "Don't let that concern you, Miss Morris. I did actually manage before you were first hired. And you might recall," he added icily, "that it was not I who hired you to begin with."

"How very true," she agreed. "It was your mother, who has excellent taste in employees!"

"We can agree to disagree on that point," he said stiffly.

"Should you be getting back to the office, before any more files become . . . misplaced?" she hinted.

His broad face hardened even more. "Cute," he said. "Very cute. Go ahead and be a detective. That should be right up your alley, the way you mind everyone's business but your own!"

"Somebody needs to mind yours!" she raged. "That dizzy blonde is just out for what she can get from you—"

"She gets plenty," he interrupted hotly. "*In* bed and out," he added deliberately, his eyes piercing as if he knew how she felt and wanted to sink the knife in as far as possible.

He succeeded. It went straight to the heart. But Kit had years of practice at hiding her deeper feelings from him. She just stared at him without reacting at all, except for the sudden whiteness of her face.

The stare got to him. He felt like a fool. It wasn't a feeling he particularly enjoyed, especially with Dane and Tess standing there trying not to laugh.

"I'll get back to my office, then," he said. "Let me have the bill when you find my mother, Dane," he added as he turned. He didn't look at Kit, either.

Kit stuck her full lower lip out as she glared after his broad back. He was as big as a house, she thought irritably. All muscle and temper. If only he'd trip on his way through the door!

"If looks could kill," Tess murmured dryly.

"You couldn't kill him with a look," Kit said wearily. "It would take a bomb. And even that wouldn't hurt him if it *hit him in the head!*" she shouted after him.

He didn't react at all, which only made her madder. The door closed behind him with a thump.

"In all the years you and Tess have been friends, I've never seen you lose your temper until Logan fired you," Dane remarked. "I thought you worshiped your boss."

"His feet melted," she grumbled. "What do you want me to do this afternoon, boss?" she asked brightly, changing the subject.

"You heard what I told Logan. Find Tansy."

She groaned. "But Mrs. Deverell disappears without a trace at least two times a month," she protested. "She always turns up."

"Usually in the hospital or in jail," he reminded her, chuckling. "Logan's mother is a dyed-in-the-wool troublemaker with a fatal philosophy of life."

"Yes. 'If it feels good, do it,'" Tess quoted. "The agency stays solvent because of Tansy's wanderlust."

"Last time she was missing, she started a riot in Newport News, Virginia, claiming to have been kidnapped by a flying saucer," Dane recalled. "We bailed her out of a sanitarium." He laughed. "Tansy just likes to start trouble. She's no lunatic."

"Most seventy-year-old women have the good sense to stay home. Tansy is a renegade. And she may not be a lunatic, but she does act like one," Tess said. "Didn't she go sailboarding in Miami year before last and pick up some middle-eastern potentate who wanted her to join his harem?"

"Yes. And we had to practically kidnap her to get her away from him, to Tansy's dismay. But as they sometimes say, all the wrong people are locked up. Tansy is a breath of fresh air. A totally uninhibited free soul."

"Her son isn't," Kit said.

"Logan's straitlaced. But Christopher Deverell isn't," Dane said. "Chris is as nutty as his mother, and both of them love to get Logan behind the eight ball."

"In other words," Tess said, reading her husband's mind, "this could be a deliberate disappearance. If Tansy knew he'd fired you, this might be her way of getting even. She did like you."

"Always," Kit agreed, smiling as she recalled how well they got along. She suspected Tansy knew how she felt about Logan, too. But remembering it wasn't going to help things, it only made her sad for what her life was like without her temperamental boss.

She missed the silliest things. She missed the way he spilled coffee on his important papers and raised the roof, yelling for her as if she was salvation itself when she came running with a roll of paper towels. She missed evenings when she accompanied him to dinners. It was usually to take notes, and strictly business, but it felt good to wear her prettiest clothes and be in the company of a man who had a mind like a steel-trap and still looked devastating in a dinner jacket.

"Kit?"

Tess's query brought her mind back to the present. "Sorry. I was thinking about where to start looking for Tansy."

"Call Chris first," Dane suggested. "Meanwhile, I'm taking Mrs. Lassiter to lunch."

"Actually we're taking lunch to the baby." Tess chuckled. "I'm still breast-feeding. Don't mind if we're a little late. I hate having to leave him at all during the day, even if he is five months old."

"I think I'd feel the same way," Kit said.

They left and she watched them, faintly envious of the way they seemed to belong together. She'd wanted that with Logan Deverell, but he wanted his scheming lady friend. He was going to get taken to the cleaners, did he but know it, and Kit wasn't going to be around to mop him up anymore. If he spilled coffee, or even tears, somebody else would have that chore. She wasn't sorry, she told herself, she wasn't sorry at all.

She went to work at once. Her first call was, as Dane had suggested, to Christopher Deverell.

"Mother's gone again," he said pleasantly. He was only twenty-seven, just two years older than Kit—but eight years younger than Logan. He and Kit and Tansy were like a different generation. Nobody ever told Logan that, of course.

"Yes, I know, that's why I'm calling you," Kit said with a smile in her tone. "I have to find her."

"Logan's office is a mess," he said. "Logan screamed bloody murder for two solid days and refused to hire anybody else."

"I know," she said. "I was due for a change. I was stagnating in that office with the same routine day in and day out—"

"Bull," Chris said. "You were eaten up with jealousy over the delectable Miss Corley. Everybody knows how you feel about Logan, Kit. Everybody except Logan."

She didn't bother to deny it. Chris knew her too well. "He's going to marry her."

"So he says. He'll find her out in time, though. Logan's no fool. Well, most of the time he's no fool."

"She's very pretty."

"So are you."

"I'm just a walking piece of office furniture that he programmed to do his filing and typing," Kit said solemnly. "He doesn't miss me. He's already found a replacement. Three of them, in fact."

"Mother found him the best one. She's a cousin of ours who used to live in San Antonio, and she can type. The other two...well," he said noncommittally. "Let's just say that they aren't quite what he had in mind. Melody, that's our cousin, is the best of them all, but she can't spell and she's very nervous trying to answer the telephone."

"I would be, too, with a glowering boss peering down his nose at me," Kit muttered. "Don't you have other relatives in San Antonio?" she asked, remembering some veiled references to people Logan didn't ever go and visit there.

"Just Emmett. Don't *ever* mention Emmett to Logan," he added. "He has nightmares about his last visit there."

"I won't see Logan to mention anybody to him, thank God," she said curtly.

"You hope. Logan isn't coping well without you," he said gently. "He won't admit it, but life without you is like going around in a blindfold."

"I hope he trips over a potted plant and goes out the window."

"Naughty, naughty," he chided. "Don't you feel guilty, leaving him at the mercy of an office you're not in?"

"No. It's time he knew what the real world is like," Kit said.

"From the tidbits I get from Melody, he may try to toss the new receptionist out a window one day soon."

"Then I hope you know a good lawyer to defend him. I'll be a character witness for the woman. Just call me."

"Shame on you!" He laughed.

"I hate your brother. I gave him three of the best years of my life and he never even noticed I was around until I told him his new girlfriend was a miner who'd be digging for gold in his hip pocket."

"You should have told Tansy instead. She'd have handled that."

"No, she wouldn't," Kit argued. "Tansy doesn't believe in interfering. She thinks people should make their own mistakes. She's right, too," she muttered. "When he loses his home, his car and his business to his heartthrob, I'm going to phone him twice a day just to say I told you so!"

"Before or after you offer to take dictation for free to help him get back on his feet?"

She sighed. Chris knew her too well. ''Where do you think Tansy's gone?''

''To Venice,'' he said. ''She was seen boarding a plane bound for there in Miami.''

''Okay. Which airline?''

He told her, along with the flight number and time of departure. She thanked him, cutting off the conversation before he could say anything else. She turned her attention to the task at hand. She had no time to wallow in self-pity.

Minutes later, she knew that Tansy Deverell had bought a ticket to Venice. But the woman who boarded the plane wasn't Tansy. Whoever Logan's cunning mother had gotten to take her place had forgotten to limp as she walked down the concourse. Tansy limped just temporarily because of an accident while she was hang gliding.

Kit laughed. She had to be a natural, just as Dane had said. She was getting the hang of this in a big way. She went back to talk to the skip tracers. They were masters at the game of invention to get information, and most of them could find a needle in a haystack within five minutes.

Unfortunately Tansy was harder to find than a needle. They drew a blank.

''I'm sorry,'' Doris said, shaking her head. ''But she's harder to find than a white bear in a snowstorm. If she paid someone to take her place on that flight, she did it with cash. You'll have to find a flight attendant to ask for a description, and even then, it won't be easy. Those flights to Venice are usually full. Individual faces are hard to remember.''

Kit could have ground her teeth. "What do I do?" she moaned. "Dane will fire me!"

"Oh, not yet," Doris said, smiling. "He never fires anyone before Friday."

"Thanks a lot."

"I did get you the name of a cabdriver at the airport who remembers an elderly lady with a limp." Doris chuckled, handing her a slip of paper.

"You angel!"

"No kissing," Doris said, warding her off. "You'll give Adams ideas," she added with a covert glance at the burly Adams, who was playing with a penknife two desks in front of her.

"There's not a thing wrong with Adams," Kit said, smiling. "He's a doll."

Adams overheard her and perked up. He got up, straightening his tie, and smiled in Kit's direction.

"He has homing instincts. You'll be sorry," Doris said under her breath.

"How about lunch, Kit?" Adams drawled with a hopeful smile.

"I'd love it, Adams," she replied, "but I have to go track down a cabdriver. Rain check?"

He brightened. He blushed. No woman in the office had *ever* offered him a rain check. He lost ten years and his morose expression. Doris studied him with renewed interest.

"Rain check," he agreed.

Doris toyed with her pen. "I'm not doing anything for lunch," she said to herself.

Adams thought he might have a heart attack. *Two* women found him interesting in less than two minutes. Maybe his luck was finally changing. Kit was pretty, and petite Doris was adorable, even with salt-and-pepper hair and glasses. "How about a chicken burger, Doris?" he asked quickly. "I'll buy!"

Doris beamed at him. "I'd love that!"

Kit eased out the door with relief and delight. Doris and Adams were both middle-aged loners with no family to speak of. Why hadn't anyone ever thought of tossing them together?

That made her think of salads, and she remembered that she hadn't had any lunch. Thanks to Logan Deverell, she'd probably starve. If she didn't die of pneumonia from standing around in wet clothes. First, she was going home to change and eat a sandwich. Then she'd find that cabbie.

Two

Kit found the cabdriver without great difficulty. Yes, he did remember an elderly woman with a limp. He'd taken her to the bus station.

With fervent thanks, Kit rushed over to the bus station. One of the ticket agents remembered a silver-haired woman with a limp. She'd taken a bus to San Antonio.

Kit groaned. She shouldn't have taken time to change clothes and eat lunch. By the time she could get to San Antonio, Tansy would be long gone.

She went back to the office, downcast and gloomy, to tell Dane what she'd found out.

"Chris mentioned a relative in San Antonio named Emmett, but I don't know if he's got the same last name as Logan and Chris."

But Dane only grinned. "No problem," he said. "I've got a contact in San Antonio who owes me a favor. This will be a great time to collect."

"Will I need to go out there?" she asked hesitantly.

"Of course not. Logan only wants to know where she is. We won't be obliged to follow her. Not yet, anyway," he added with a knowing smile.

Kit was given a new assignment, one which wasn't quite as interesting as trying to find an elderly needle in a haystack. A man wanted his wife followed to see if she was two-timing him. This was relatively easy for Kit to do, especially since the woman seemed bent on a shopping spree.

Staying a little behind the woman, Kit was just congratulating herself on her stealth when Logan Deverell loomed up in her path and brought her to a standstill.

"Where is the Dawson file?" he demanded. "Some private detective you are, you can't even put things in their proper place!"

Kit could have hit him. The woman she'd been shadowing couldn't possibly have missed hearing her loud ex-boss denouncing her. Sure enough, the woman gave her a startled glance and dived toward the nearest cab.

"There, look what you've done," Kit cried, exasperated. "I'm on a case! I was shadowing a client, for heaven's sake . . . !"

"I want the Dawson file," he said. "None of those would-be secretaries have any idea how to find it. You've got to come back with me. I'm going to lose my most influential client if you don't."

"I should *care?*" she burst out.

He glowered down at her. His dark eyes narrowed with irritation. "You're costing me time," he muttered, slamming back the immaculate white cuff of his shirt so that he could see the gold watch imbedded in the thick, curling black hair on his muscular wrist.

"I was on a case," she pointed out. "*You* hijacked me. Speaking of hijacking—"

He was pulling her along as she spoke. "Can't you be quiet for two minutes running?" he asked conversationally. "All you need to do is find a file. What's so difficult about that?"

While she was trying to formulate it in words of one syllable that he might be able to understand, he helped her into his gray Lincoln.

I'm crazy, that's what I am, Kit thought as he got in under the wheel. *He's blown an assignment for me, fired me, humiliated me and here I am letting him lead me to his office to work for him on my own time!* Well, actually, she admitted it was on Dane's time.

"Have you found my mother yet?" he asked as he pulled away from the curb.

"We're working on it," she said.

He cocked a busy eyebrow. "I thought you were in charge of the case?"

"I am. But I lost her at the bus station."

He chuckled. "My mother wouldn't be caught dead on a bus."

"She would and did, to escape surveillance. Doesn't she have a relative named Emmett in San Antonio?" she persisted, remembering only then that Chris had warned her never to mention him.

"Oh, yes," he said with a vicious glare. "Emmett lives in San Antonio, as near as not. But I guarantee she wouldn't go there. Nobody in the family will go near the place. You'd have to be out of your ever-loving mind to want to go and see Emmett, even if you were hiding out from the police!"

The man must be a holy terror, she thought. He was Logan's cousin, of course. Probably it ran in the family.

"Where does he live?" she asked, and whipped out a pad and pen.

"I told you, she wouldn't go there!"

"Humor me."

He shrugged. "His name is E. G. Deverell." He gave her the address. She jotted it down and stuck the pad back into her purse. Now she had something concrete to go on. She felt like a real detective.

"You can't really like following people around for a living," he said. He glanced at her and back at the road. "I've bought a new computer for the office. It's got a sixty megabyte hard drive and all sorts of software, including a user-friendly word processing program. I bought a laser printer, too," he added. "And the system does forms."

She'd been begging for that sort of system for over a year. He'd argued that it wasn't necessary and he had better ways to spend his money.

"How nice," she said. "For your *new* secretary. Secretaries, that is," she added with a spiteful smile. "Three, isn't it?"

He made a rough sound under his breath. "I don't see what your problem is!" he raged. "I've lost my temper with you before. You never walked out on me!''

''You never allowed one of your women to treat me like an indentured servant before,'' she countered.

He shifted uncomfortably. ''She asked for a cup of coffee.''

''Excuse me,'' she said. ''She *demanded* a cup of coffee, and then threw it at me because it was too strong. When I suggested that she might like to go to the restaurant on the first floor and get a cup there, she flew into a rage and called me several names that I won't repeat. Then, the minute she saw you coming, she dissolved into helpless tears.''

''She said you threw the coffee at her,'' he returned, narrowing one eye. ''And you aren't the most even-tempered of women.''

''Oh, but I am, as long as I'm not within half a mile of you,'' she replied venomously.

He had to stifle a smile at the way she was looking at him. How he'd missed these bouts with Kit. The three women he'd had to hire to replace her were frightened of him. Poor Melody was hopelessly intimidated by spelling, and her distant cousin Logan. She could type very quickly, though, and she was efficient.

Harriet, the tallest of the three, could file and do payroll accounts, but she hated everyone in the office and smoked like a chimney.

Then there was Margo, who spelled like a dictionary and wanted nothing more than to seduce him.

Logan, though, had eyes for no one except Betsy, who made his blood run hot and wild through his veins. He didn't want to get married, but it was the only way he was ever going to possess the delectable Betsy. So he'd given in, against his better judgment, and nothing had gone right in his life since he'd proposed. He was no nearer to coaxing Betsy into his bed and he'd lost Kit. Amazing, he thought, how empty the world was without Kit in it. He had no one to talk to anymore. Betsy hardly listened to him, and certainly paid more attention to where they went and who they saw than what they did.

"Betsy was no threat to your job," he told her. "I don't combine my personal relationships with my business ones. I thought you knew that."

She knew that he was going to marry Betsy, and she couldn't bear it. Not only was she losing the only man she'd ever loved, but she was losing him to a woman who'd cut his heart out and roast it over a pile of blazing hundred-dollar bills. Betsy would take him for every cent he had. She glanced over at him curiously. How, she wondered, could a man with a brain such as his be so terminally stupid when it came to women?

"You aren't going to be happy working in a detective agency," he persisted.

"But I am," she corrected. She smiled smugly. "I'm treated like a person there. When I do something right, I get praised for it. When I do something wrong," she added with a meaningful look, "nobody rages at me in disgusting language and threatens to feed me my handbag."

"How boring."

She smothered a laugh and looked away.

"You miss me, damn you," he murmured, smiling at her averted face. "Our daily battles kept you going when nothing else did. You loved trying to get one up on me. Remember the day the Brazilian businessmen came to the office and you spent thirty minutes trying to speak Spanish to them?"

"*You* told me they spoke it."

"*You* should have known that the national language of Brazil is Portuguese. Anyway, you got even."

"Indeed I did," she recalled with a grin. "I borrowed one of the girls from the secretarial pool who spoke no English and sent her in to take dictation from you while I took a two-hour lunch break."

"I almost broke your neck," he said shortly. "She sat there and nodded and smiled at me for thirty minutes before I realized that she didn't understand a word I said."

"The girls in the next office did." She chuckled. "They said you were very eloquent. In fact, one of them wanted to have you arrested."

"The good old days," he said wistfully. He glared at her. "Now I have two helpers who get down on their knees and thank God when I leave the office, and a third who spends her life trying to bend me back over my own desk."

"Oh, my," she said.

"You might pretend to be sympathetic. It's uncomfortable to work in that kind of environment."

"Now you know how women feel," she replied.

He glared at her. "I don't recall ever chasing you around the office or trying to bend you over a desk!"

More's the pity, she wanted to say. But she only replied, "No, sir, you never did."

"Do you know, I've actually thought about reporting her for harassment?"

"If she makes you that uncomfortable, why not just fire her?"

"Because she can spell, Morris." He exploded. "She can spell! That's something neither of the others can do!"

"You could ask the agency to send you someone with good spelling skills."

"I did," he replied tersely. "They sent me Margo of the peekaboo bosom."

She put her face in her hands, but she couldn't stem the laughter.

"Come back," he invited roughly. "I'll give you a raise. You can have a new desk. I'll fix the damned window that sticks."

"I'm very tempted," she said, and meant it. But she'd never be able to stomach Betsy at close range. "But I like my new job too much to quit now."

"I hope Dane isn't assigning you anything dangerous."

"Now, see here," she began defensively.

"Here we are!" He stopped the car, helped her out and escorted her into the building and up the elevator to his office.

"Now," he said, opening the door for her. "Find that file!"

She blinked twice before she walked into the luxurious carpeted office. The spot where Betsy had thrown coffee at her three weeks before was still there.

No one had come to clean it up. The coffeemaker was standing empty and very dirty. Three desks were piled high with file folders and stacks of correspondence. Diskettes for the computer were lying around, out of their jackets. One of the women had gray hair and was very tall. She was smoking and her ashes were everywhere. Another was talking on the telephone, apparently to someone male. She smiled at Logan and deliberately leaned forward to show her cleavage.

"Hello, Margo," Kit said sweetly.

"Hi! How did you know my name?" the girl replied, and suddenly went back to the voice on the other end of the line.

"Cute," Logan muttered.

Kit walked toward the third desk, the only neat one, where a third woman, plain and harassed-looking, was flipping through files.

"Not yet, I'm afraid," she told Logan in an apprehensive tone. She looked about twenty, a country-looking girl with a patent vulnerability in her face, and Kit felt a surge of sympathy for her.

"Here, let me help," Kit said kindly. Laying aside her purse, she bent over the stack and in seconds, extricated the one Logan had demanded. "Here."

He took it and glared at the young woman.

"How could I know that it would be filed under Portfolios?" she asked plaintively. "I'm new...!"

"I'm Kit Morris." Kit introduced herself.

"I'm Melody Cartman," came the reply. She glanced toward Logan, who was making a telephone call. "You used to work here, didn't you? No wonder you left! See Harriet over there? She'd stopped smoking for ten years when she came to work here. Now she's gone back. She's smoking three packs a day, and she's got a bottle of Scotch in her desk!"

"I can understand why," Kit mused. Logan, buried in his file, hadn't noticed them discussing him.

"Margo isn't afraid of him. She likes men. Especially rich ones. He has a girlfriend and she's terrible. She expects us to stop everything and wait on her. Not to his face, of course," she muttered. "She's sweetness and light the minute he walks in the door."

"Now you know why I don't work here anymore."

"He's my third cousin," Melody groaned, glancing at him. "He's just like one other terrible member of the family. If I'd had any idea he was like this, I'd never have let Tansy talk me into this job. But the company I worked for went bust and I just couldn't bear to go back to San Antonio." She hesitated. "I'm stuck here!"

"Listen," Kit said, raising her voice, "we're short one detective at the agency where I work . . ."

"Shut up, Morris," Logan said menacingly as he slammed the telephone receiver back onto the cradle. "You aren't stealing any of my people."

He moved away and Melody groaned. "See? We're slaves. He owns us! I'll never see my apartment again . . . !"

"There, there, it will be all right. I'll take a few minutes and explain my filing system to you. Then you won't have this problem again."

Melody dabbed at her brown eyes and pushed back her thick, blond-streaked light brown hair. It was very long, and she had a sweetly rounded face and freckles. Kit liked her at once. "I think Harriet carries one of those electrical weapons in her purse," Melody told Kit. "Wouldn't you like to borrow it? You could do him in before you leave. I swear to God, none of us would ever tell on you!"

Kit chuckled. "I believe you, but he's really not worth the sacrifice. Let's get to work."

It only took thirty minutes to teach Melody the basics of the filing system, and then Kit gave Melody her telephone number for future emergencies.

"He doesn't like you to know it," Kit added, "but there's a smokeless ashtray in the closet. Two of them, in fact. He used to smoke cigars."

"He doesn't smoke cigars any more."

"I know."

"He smokes cigarettes now. Thin brown ones."

"Marijuana?" Kit exclaimed.

Melody laughed. "Oh, no. Those little cigars, what do they call them? Cigarillos, I think!"

"Not in here, I hope?"

"Yes. Between him and Harriet, I'm a stretcher case with my sinuses."

"Use those ashtrays."

Melody brightened. "If I suggest it, maybe he'll fire me!"

"You needn't look so optimistic. Now that you know my filing system, you're worth your weight in rubies."

"Drat!"

"If you can become an ace speller, he'll get rid of Margo," she whispered.

Melody's eyes twinkled. "I'll hire a tutor!"

"Good luck!"

Kit walked into Logan's office as she had for the past three years, without knocking. But she realized at once that she'd made a mistake.

Somehow, Betsy must have gotten into the office while she was occupied with Melody. Betsy was there now, blond and fragile, in Logan's arms.

The sight of them that way made something delicate inside Kit go brittle and shatter. Logan's dark head bent over that bright one, his enormous body sheltering hers, his arms compelling her against the powerful length of him, his mouth devouring and insistent on the woman's lips.

He lifted his head abruptly and looked at Kit with the desire and physical enslavement still glittering in his dark eyes.

"Well?" he asked huskily.

Kit didn't say a word. She turned and closed the door behind her, trying not to remember the snide look on Betsy's exultant face as she went. That had been a setup. Betsy knew how she felt about Logan. Everyone knew, except Logan himself.

She gathered her purse and said a quick goodbye to Melody, pausing only to wave at Margo and Harriet before she walked to the elevator.

The stupid conveyance *would* be on the bottom floor, she muttered to herself. She jabbed viciously at the Down button and was almost resigned to going down the staircase when Logan and Betsy came along to stand beside her.

"We'll drop you off," Logan said carelessly. "We have a luncheon appointment."

Kit looked from Betsy, immaculate in a gray silk suit and an ermine coat, to Logan in his blue pin-striped suit and handmade silk tie. Yes, they complimented each other. She'd been living in a fool's paradise to imagine a man such as Logan would ever give her a second look. She was a teacher's daughter with no special beauty or talents. He was related to royalty somewhere in his ancestry and had gobs of money. She held Betsy in contempt for coveting his status and wealth, but he'd probably think that Kit was eager for it as well if she'd ever tempted him deliberately as Margo and Betsy had.

Just as well, she thought, that she'd been allowed to get out when she did. Soon, she'd never have to see Logan again. Betsy would make sure of that.

"I do hope you haven't been trying to tell Logan any of that silly gossip about me," Betsy drawled with a cool smile. "I don't chase men for money. I don't have to. I have money of my own."

Certainly she did. Bill Kingsley's money. Kit's blood ran hot every time she thought about the poor, kind old man. He must have been easy pickings indeed for this blond toad. And here was Logan, waiting in line to be next.

"Some women do chase men for money, though," Kit said quietly. She studied the other woman with cold curiosity. "One of my neighbors was chased after he won a lottery. His name was Bill Kingsley."

Betsy's face whitened. She averted it. "I'm afraid I don't know anyone by that name."

"Well, you wouldn't," Kit said easily. "He used to live in my apartment building, about the time he won the small lottery."

"You said he did live in your building? I suppose he left when he won the money?" Betsy asked with assumed politeness, but an underlying nervousness that was visible.

"He left, all right. The lottery wasn't too much, but it was more than he'd ever had. When he found out, he celebrated by buying drinks for everyone at the bar around the corner. That was where he met a young woman who started being nice to him and let him take her around. She was young and pretty and he was a lonely old man with no family. He fell in love with her. She repaid him for his kindness by taking him for every penny he had. She even managed to cost him his savings. After she left, he couldn't believe he'd been such a fool. He simply couldn't live with it. He committed suicide." Kit shook her head, her eyes never leaving Betsy's paper-white face. "If I were that woman, I'd choke on my own greed. And I'd deserve to."

"None of that has anything to do with Betsy!" Logan said angrily.

"No, of course not," Kit replied, smiling at him. "Did I say that it had?"

"It's all right, Logan," Betsy said, having regained her composure if not her color. "You and I have so much, and poor Kit has nothing. Not even a man's love."

Touché, Kit thought. Betsy gave her a smile that would have curled leather.

"Where can we drop you, dear?" Betsy purred.

"I wouldn't want to take you out of your way. I'll just pop onto a bus downstairs. Do have a lovely lunch. Ta, ta." Kit smiled and waltzed to the staircase.

"Morris, come back here . . . !"

She ignored the demand and kept going. She was shaking inside with rage at Betsy's blatant playacting. The woman was as guilty as sin and felt no remorse at all. She was going to cut Logan up just the way she'd cut up Kingsley. And how was Kit going to stop her? In Logan's eyes, Betsy could do no wrong. But there had to be a way to stop Betsy and save him in time!

She worried the question all the way back to the office, where she had to explain to Dane what had happened.

"I'm sorry," Dane apologized when he could finally stop laughing. "But that's such a dandy little tale . . ."

"It's the truth!" Kit threw up her hands. "He's my nemesis, I tell you! And one of his very own employees—his third cousin, in fact!—offered me an electrical device and said she'd swear I was innocent if I'd just bump him off for them!"

. "Kit, are you sure you've done the right thing to leave an office like that?" he asked her. "Logan is never going to be the same again."

"Good. I hope Margo gets him pregnant."

"Stop that!" He leaned forward and picked up a notepad, whipping off a sheet. "Well I can solve your problems for a day or so. Take this."

"What is it?" she murmured, reading a street address.

"Emmett's address. Get on the next flight to San Antonio and follow these directions. They should lead you right to Tansy Deverell."

"Hallelujah! I'll kidnap her and send Logan a ransom note...."

"Not while you're on my payroll, please."

"It was just a thought." She folded the note. "I'm sorry about losing the lady I was trailing for you."

"That was hardly your fault. It's okay."

She shrugged, fingering the note. "I seem to get in deeper all the time. I had a neighbor who Betsy Corley took for everything he had." She looked up. "She'll do that to Logan, you know. He's so besotted he won't believe a bad thing about her. She'll lead him right to the slaughter and make him think he's heaven-bound. Just like she did poor old Bill."

"You don't give Logan credit for having much sense, do you?" he asked gently.

She shrugged. "How can I? After all, he sacrificed three years of loyal, slavish devotion and adoration over a cup of spilled coffee, didn't he?"

"He was an idiot there," Dane had to agree. "I'm sorry you've had such a rough deal. Maybe this job will open new doors for you."

She smiled. "Maybe it will. Do you know any more about this address besides its location?"

"Just that Tansy's nephew is something of a hell-raiser. He and Tansy should get along just fine."

"Another Chris," she said, shaking her head.

"Well...not exactly," he replied slowly. "Never mind, just go out there and find out. And, if you get in trouble or have any problems, any at all, just phone here and I'll demand that you come right home to work on another case. Okay?"

That sounded very much as if he were keeping something from her. She wondered what. Her eyebrows lifted. "Now I'm intrigued."

"You will be. That's a promise." He chuckled. "From what we ferreted out, intrigued is an understatement for what most people think when they meet Emmett."

She put a hand on her hip. "Emmett?"

"Well, most people don't call him that if they want to stay out of emergency rooms. Better make it Mr. Deverell until you know him."

"Should I invest in one of those electrical devices...?"

"Doris will have your ticket."

"Yes, sir." She saluted and walked out. Sure enough, Doris was waving it at her when she approached. Adams was nearby, grinning.

"Don't get involved with the natives," Doris told her. "Those San Antonio men are tornadoes when you get them wound up."

"I'll try to remember that. See you when I can. Goodbye, Adams," she added, waving at him and smiling.

Adams seemed to gain height and masculine beauty as he grinned back.

"Hands off," Doris whispered. "He's all mine."

She said it just loud enough that Adams could hear it, which made his smile even broader. "Good luck," she whispered back to Doris. And with a wave of her hand, she went to get the necessary things out of her desk before she left for her trip.

San Antonio was big. It boasted a million in population and some of the most interesting things to see and do in the country, including the Alamo and the Paseo Del Rio.

Before she went searching for the address and directions in her purse, she checked into the nearest hotel and took time to get a bite of lunch and rest.

Then she got into her rental car and set out for the address Dane had given her.

It was on the southeastern side of town, and not in a subdivision. In fact, the address was something of a ranch, complete with oil wells pumping in the pastures and white fences all around. Red-coated cattle grazed in thickets of mesquite, past flatland that had patches of prickly pear cactus to hallmark it.

She looked at the address a second time to be sure, but there it was. No one had ever said that the Deverells had a cattle-raising relative out here in Texas.

As she drove across the cattle grate and down the long, winding dirt driveway to the elegant two-story Victorian house in the distance, she was suddenly assailed by three war-painted buckskin-clad midgets with bows and arrows and chicken-feather warbonnets.

"Hold it right there, palefacette," one of them drawled "You're our captive."

She shouldn't have stopped, she supposed, but they'd looked so cute! Now they looked menacing and ferocious—if you could call grammar school kids dangerous.

They all looked like boys, but one of them turned out to be a girl. They piled into the back seat and commanded Kit to drive.

"We're the Deverell gang," the spokesperson said. "I'm Guy. That's Polk. She's Amy."

"Yes, we're the reason our daddy can't get married." Polk piped up. "We're savages, like our lus... illl... us..."

"Illustrious," Amy said for him.

"Thanks! Illustrious ancestors, that is," Polk continued.

"They were Comanches!" Amy whispered.

"One of them, Amy, only one," Polk muttered, "and she was our three-times great-grandmother. For heaven's sake...!"

"You said we were Indians," Amy persisted. "That's why we're wearing these silly costumes!"

"It's Thanksgiving in two days," came the reply from the spokesman, Guy. "And we're in a school play tomorrow, which is Monday, so we're rehearsing."

"We're going to kidnap the principal, Mr. Deere, and hold him for ransom!"

I like these kids, Kit thought. *They're my kind of people. I wonder if they know anything about kidnapping financial experts?*

"Stop here," Guy said. "And don't try anything funny, pilgrim."

Amy leaned toward him. "Pilgrimette," she corrected.

As John Wayne impersonations went, it left a lot to be desired, but it wasn't too bad, considering. Smothering a laugh, Kit got out of the car and raised her hands as three ferocious Native Americans with bows raised herded her toward the porch and the front door.

"Knock!" Guy said.

She did. There was the muffled, quick and heavy sound of footsteps approaching and a deep voice asking some kind of question. The door opened, and Kit looked up, way up, to a muscular jean-clad body into the palest green eyes in the most unwelcoming darkly tanned face she'd ever seen in her life.

"Well, I'll be damned," he murmured thoughtfully, glancing at his brood. "Another captive! Bring her in, boys, and we'll build a nice warm fire."

The last thing Kit saw before she hit the floor was the surprise that momentarily softened those fierce features.

Three

———

Kit opened her eyes and there was that lean, dark face again. White teeth gleamed in it. Green eyes glittered humorously in it.

"Welcome back," a deep voice said.

"You can't burn me at the stake," Kit said in a rush.

"Beg pardon?"

"Move, Emmett," an elderly voice said stridently. "Don't be absurd, Kit," Tansy Deverell chuckled, "of course he isn't going to burn you at the stake. I tell you, Emmett, these children are even worse than you were at their ages! You've got to do something about them!"

"You want us to go away, don't you?" Guy asked belligerently. "Well, we won't! This is our house, and we can stay here if we want. Tell her, Dad."

"I can't argue with the boy. Look, he's armed," Emmett said reasonably, gesturing toward the bow Guy was holding.

"You're his father!" Tansy raged.

Emmett frowned and looked at Guy and then at Polk and finally at Amy. "That's what their mother said." He sighed. "I guess they do look like me. Lady, are you all right?" he asked, remembering Kit, who was sitting up dizzily.

"Yes, I'm just getting over the shock. It isn't every day you get captured by a band of Indians and threatened with the stake."

"Aw, gee, lady, we wouldn't have burned you," Polk said. "It's a lot of work to cut that much wood."

Kit stared at him blankly.

"Why did you faint?" Tansy asked curtly, her blue eyes somber in a lovely complexion that hadn't aged, with a frame of beautifully groomed silver hair. "Has my son gotten you in trouble?" she added angrily.

"I'm not pregnant," Kit muttered. "And if I was, it would make biological history. Your son is much too busy getting himself married to one of the world's prime gold diggers."

"Yes, I know," Tansy said wistfully. "He wouldn't listen to me, either. I'm sorry he fired you, Kit. He'll be sorry, too."

"No, he won't. He replaced me." She grinned at Tansy. "It only took him three women to do it. One can do payroll and filing, but she carries an electric weapon and smokes like a furnace. One can spell, but she's trying to seduce him. And the third one could do all three if she wasn't scared to death of him. She's nice."

"That would be Melody," Tansy said, and bit her tongue at the quick, almost violent look Emmett gave her.

"Melody?" he asked slowly. "Melody Cartman?"

"Yes, that's her name," Kit said, too shaken to notice the undercurrents. "If the smoke doesn't kill her, she might work out to be his right hand someday."

"I hate cigarettes," Tansy said with a pointed look at Emmett.

"Cigarettes are a curse," he agreed. Then he shrugged off his bad mood, grinned, pulled one out of his pocket and lit it, daring the onlookers to say a word.

"Okay, Dad. You asked for it," Guy muttered. He whipped around to his back, pulled a water pistol, and quickly extinguished the glowing tip.

Emmett stared at it with a forlorn sigh and dropped it. "Damn. That was my last one."

"And don't try that again, partner," Guy said firmly, twirling the water pistol back into his pocket while his siblings applauded loudly. He grinned at Kit. "Hey, lady, want to come hunting rabbits with us?"

"No, thanks, I feel a bit endangered right now."

"We wouldn't have a post to tie you to out in the brush," Polk argued.

"But there's the brush itself," Amy mused. "It's very dry, and I got one of Emmett's old lighters..."

"Will you stop calling me Emmett?" he muttered at his child. "I'm your father. Show a little respect."

"Yes, Emmett," Amy said politely, pulling the lighter out of her pocket.

She flashed it and Emmett grabbed it. "Not anymore, you don't," he said. "Scat, you varmints! And don't bring back any rattlers this time!"

They scampered out, giggling and murmuring among themselves while Kit caught her breath.

"Nobody in the family ever comes here," Tansy said as she and Emmett helped Kit up. "Can you *guess* why?" she added with a pointed glare at Emmett.

"I could probably make a stab at it," Kit mused.

"He's spoiled them rotten. They don't do anything they don't want to. The only exception he made was school. He insisted that they get educated."

"So I won't have to support them for the rest of my life," Emmett explained. He looked down at Kit and measured her with his glittering green eyes. "How do you feel about brief engagements? We could get married right after lunch."

Kit stared at him. "What?"

"I guess you're one of those girls who believe in long engagements, aren't you? Okay. We can wait until tomorrow to get married, then."

"He does this all the time," Tansy said sadly, shaking her head. "Pay him no attention."

"That's the trouble, nobody does!" Emmett said in exasperation, throwing up his hands. "I've been turned down five times in one month." He narrowed one eye, and glanced at Kit. "Maybe my luck's changing, though. You're not bad on the eyes and you can type. You could handle those kids and help me out in the office, too. We could be a ranching family.

Think of it," he said with a gleam in his eyes, "we could found a dynasty here. Several more kids and a few good bulls..."

"Wait a minute, please," Kit said, putting out a hand. "I have just avoided becoming a human sacrifice once today. You really will have to seek a soul mate elsewhere. I have it in mind to become the female Charlie Chan."

"Another private eye." He shook his head. "What is it with you women and trench coats? We had a female private eye down here just a couple of months ago, looking for a missing woman." He glanced toward the door. "Those kids again. They nabbed her at a rest stop and tied her to a tree. Good thing the fire attracted attention from the highway."

Kit didn't dare ask any more. She simply stood and stared at him as if she doubted his sanity and her own. "Do you often send your children out to hijack prospective brides, Mr. Deverell?"

"They won't go at all if I don't pay them, the mercenary little devils," he told her outrageously. "They say I'm too cheap to get a really good woman. I don't know, though, you're pretty easy on the eyes. How about it? I've got all my own teeth." He grinned to show them.

"Thank you, but I don't want to marry you."

"Of course not. You don't know me yet. I'll court you over barbecued ribs." He frowned. "You do like barbecue? I simply couldn't marry a woman who didn't."

She chuckled at the sheer absurdity of it. "Yes, I like barbecue."

"You can't marry her," Tansy said firmly. "I've got her all staked out for my son."

"I don't like Chris that much," Kit said demurely.

"You know I wasn't talking about Chris," Tansy murmured.

"*He* likes the beauteous Betsy," came the terse reply.

"Excuse me, but the two of you are talking about Cousin Logan, aren't you?" Emmett asked. "What's he gotten himself into this time?"

Tansy told him while Kit listened.

Emmett shook his head. "It runs in the family. All us Deverells are fools when it comes to women. Look at me. My ex-wife couldn't wait to marry me so we could have kids. But when we started having them, she got tired of it, so she ran off with a damned mechanic." His eyes narrowed with feeling. "Go figure."

"Didn't your wife ever want to come back?" Kit asked.

He shrugged. "She called a while back, but I lost the telephone number. It's just as well," he added, for an instant, there was something not at all easygoing in the glint of his green eyes. "She got *tired* of the kids...God!"

"There are women in the world who just aren't cut out for motherhood, Emmett," Tansy said. "There are others who would love your brood. Or at least there would be, if your horrible reputation didn't precede you. Nobody will come near the place because of those kids, and you've encouraged them in a most unfatherly way to be hooligans."

"Straitlaced kids never have any fun, Tansy." He chuckled. "I know. I was raised in a military academy. It took me years to shake off rules and tradition and start having fun." His eyes grew wistful. "Do you know, I've treed more bars locally than the town drunk?"

"Your sins will come back to haunt you," Tansy predicted.

"Not before I get a mother for those kids," he said. "They're going to seed."

"You planted them."

"I have to work, don't I?"

"I wouldn't call riding in every rodeo from Texas to Montana necessity. You're breaking every bone in your body one at a time."

"It takes money to keep this place going. The plumbing's half shot. I'll have to bone up on my calf-roping."

"They'd let you manage old man Ted Regan's place if you'd ask."

"Ted is only five years older than I am. He isn't even middle-aged."

"Everybody calls him old man Regan," Tansy said. "I don't know why, except that he's got prematurely silver hair. Anyway, he'd let you manage his place, but you just won't."

"I don't want to move to Houston."

"Jacobsville," Tansy corrected.

"Not much difference. And old Ted's ranch is so close to Houston that it could be called a suburb. I like San Antonio."

"It would be the best thing in the world for the kids," Tansy coaxed. "Plenty of fresh air, piney woods and green meadows, nice people."

"Girls?" he asked, lifting both eyebrows.

"Nobody is going to marry you until you civilize those children," Tansy warned.

"That's why I've got to get married. A man can't do that kind of job alone," he said plaintively. "I'm only one person, for God's sake! They outnumber me three to one!"

Kit had been listening quietly. This man was a cross between Chris and Logan. She liked him, but there seemed to be a lot more to him under the surface than was visible above it.

"You could hire a companion," she began.

He swept off his white Stetson and held it against his heart, eyes wide and stark. "Lady!" he exclaimed. "I can't bring that kind of woman into my home!"

She burst out laughing. "You're as incorrigible as Chris!"

"He taught me everything I know," he agreed. He perched the Stetson back on his head. "Yes, I suppose I could get a nursemaid for the kids, but they'd torture her to death the first night. She'd find a snake in her bed or a spider in her bath, or something even worse. I can't do that to some poor unsuspecting woman. I do have a housekeeper, though, who is away on sick leave."

"There are women who have had survival training," she said.

"I don't want a drill sergeant."

"Are you sure? Think of all the fun you'd have, watching her bring them into line," Tansy suggested.

He considered that for a minute. "No," he said finally, shaking his head. "It would break their little hearts."

"The way they're heading, they aren't going to have hearts for much longer. You've got to do something, Emmett!" Tansy said.

"Not right now. Tell us why you're here," Emmett said, turning to Kit.

"I've come to find Tansy."

Tansy's eyes widened. "Logan again!"

"He worries."

"He's a damned busybody," Tansy muttered. "My God, I can't go on a little bitty plane ride without him having me followed and reports filled out on my companions. He's terrified that I'll rewrite my will and leave all my money to someone's terrier."

"That's not true." Kit chuckled. "He's afraid you'll end up married to some twenty-year-old gigolo and kill him with sheer exhaustion."

"How flattering," the older woman said delightedly. "Emmett, do you know any twenty-year-old gigolos we could try?"

"Shame on you," he said shortly. "A nice, decent woman like you ought to be ashamed to say a thing like that to me."

"I don't know why not. Last year, you were running around with that rodeo groupie and she was spending you out of bed and board."

"She was pretty," he argued. "But the kids hated her. First time I brought her out here, she was going to go walking with them. I begged her not to, God knows I did." He shook his head. "Last time I saw her, she was fishtailing her car all over the road trying to get back to the highway, and those damned kids were rolling in the dirt laughing."

"What did they do to her?" Kit asked curiously.

"Damned if I know," he said. "They never would tell me."

"You're staying the night, aren't you, Kit?" Tansy asked.

Kit's eyes widened. "Well, no!" she stammered. "I've got a return ticket late this afternoon for Houston."

"No problem," Emmett said easily. "Hand it over and I'll get you a flight tomorrow afternoon. I'll make barbecue and serenade you with my guitar under a romantic Texas moon."

"Oh, no, not that. Anything but that!" Tansy wailed.

"Shut up," he muttered at her. "I took lessons."

"Don't sing. Trust me," Tansy said, batting her eyelashes at him.

He let out an exaggerated sigh. "Another singing career ruined by critics. Well, I'll play for you, Kit. Kit? What's it stand for?"

"I don't know," Kit said quietly. She'd never talked about her parents. The subject was much too painful, and the last person she could tell was this wild-eyed Texan. "I didn't bring a bag..."

"I'll loan you one of my pajama jackets," Emmett offered.

"You can have one of my gowns, Kit," Tansy said, elbowing a grinning Emmett out of the way. "Will you stop? Honestly, anyone would think you'd never seen a woman before!"

"Well, I haven't," he argued. "Not like this one. Chris is always ranting about how nice she is, and if you like her, that's a character reference in itself. She'd make a perfect mother for those kids."

"She's going to marry Logan one day. He just doesn't know it yet."

"I'd tell him fast if I were you, by the sounds of things."

"I wouldn't have Logan on toast!"

Emmett pursed his lips and made a whistling sound. "That sounds suspiciously like cannibalism. Speaking of cannibalism, did you know that there's fossilized evidence that *Homo erectus* was a cannibal and ate his own kind? There are smashed bones and burned bones in late Pleistocene camps..."

"Go away!" Tansy wailed. "Emmett, don't start on this poor child. She's not a prehistoric culture addict like you."

"I did a course in anthropology and I did my minor in paleontology," Emmett confessed. "Dinosaur bones, that sort of thing. Did you know that there's a fossilized link between birds and lizards? A fellow called archaeopteryx—"

"Later, later, Emmett. Now what's this about Betsy?" Tansy persisted.

Emmett watched them walk toward the living room. He could sure do worse than that sweet young thing. She was only about ten years his junior and the kids had already taken to her. For an instant, he remembered what Tansy had said about Logan's new secretary, and his blood began to burn. But he forced the thought of Melody away. He wouldn't have to see her, thank God. He never went near Logan's office. On the other hand, Kit was right here and he liked her a lot. He started whistling as he went out to feed the horses in the barn....

"Well, I won't come meekly home with you and that's that," Tansy said at supper.

"A Christian should be meek," Amy piped up. She and the boys were cleaned up, but they still looked pretty much alike. With her very short haircut, Amy could have passed for a boy.

"That's right," Kit said, smiling at the child.

Amy smiled back, and without mischief. "You're nice. Are you going to marry Emmett? We voted, and it's okay with us. You'll have to learn the rules, of course."

"Right," Guy agreed. "Bedtime is at eleven sharp. No card playing on Sunday. When Dad's got a girl in the living room, no peeking over the back of the sofa, no matter what sort of noises you hear..."

"Guy!" Emmett exploded.

"And most of all, if he's been drinking, don't get in front of him on account of he might fall on you," Amy finished.

Emmett put his hands over his face.

"You should be ashamed!" Tansy muttered, glancing at him. "Reprobate! You really are the black sheep of the family."

"He isn't black, Aunt Tansy," Polk said. "He's dirty. He always looks like that when he's been in the barn with the horses."

Kit had to wipe her mouth suddenly, but over it her eyes twinkled with unholy glee.

Emmett looked up, and the sight of those very blue eyes in merriment made him feel suddenly younger. He blinked and began to smile.

Uh-oh, Kit thought. She wiped the smile off. Here was one complication she could do without.

"You're fighting it, Kit." Emmett sighed.

"I told you, you can't have her," Tansy reminded him.

"There are plenty of women in Houston," he began.

"I've been working on this one for three years. Eat your barbecue, which is rather good, by the way. Did I ever tell you about the Russian count I met at Maxim's in Paris the last time I was there?" she added, waxing reminiscent. "He was one of the last of the Romanoffs, and he actually remembered the siege of the Winter Palace."

Emmett looked at the barbecue on his fork and began to pale.

Tansy shot a covert glance at him and continued. "There were fires everywhere. Some of the soldiers were thrown into them..."

Emmett put a hand over his mouth, dropped his food, and ran from the room.

"No guts," Guy said disgustedly, looking after him.

"Disgraceful." Polk nodded.

"Whatever are we going to do about him?" Amy sighed.

"You did it last time," Tansy reminded them while Kit sat, dumbfounded. "Bringing that...that 'not alive' thing in here on a dustpan to show him."

"Yeah," Guy chuckled. "He didn't even *make* it to the bathroom that time!"

"You ought to see him at the rodeo if there's any blood," Amy piped in. "He goes green and white, all mixed up, and his stomach churns."

"Except if it's him that's bleeding," Guy pondered. "Weird, ain't it? Never bothers him if it's his own blood. And if it's ours, and an emergency, he's never sick. But sometimes you can turn him green real easy if you talk about something yucky."

"What a terrible way to treat your poor father," Tansy chided them. But her eyes were twinkling.

When Emmett came back, his eyes were glittering with imminent retribution.

"Great barbecue, Dad. We're going in to watch that new survival show on the educational channel, okay?" Guy blabbered.

He and the others murmured excuses and ran for it.

"Little monsters!" he called after them. "I'll get you for this!"

"Why do you let them do it to you?" Tansy asked. "You know it's terminal to show weakness to children."

"Well, look who started it off," he said, narrowing his eyes at Tansy.

"Couldn't resist it," she sputtered. "You are a case, Emmett."

He picked up his fork and forced himself to eat a bite of barbecue. Amazingly it stayed down.

Kit listened to the conversation without taking part in it. This man was one of the more interesting people she'd ever met. She wondered what was going to become of him.

Logan Deverell was sitting on the doorstep of the Lassiter Detective Agency the minute it opened the next morning.

"I want to see Kit," he told Dane.

Dane lifted both eyebrows. "You can't. She's out of town running your mother to the ground."

"Where out of town?"

"San Antonio."

"Oh, no! Why in God's name did you let her go *there?*"

Dane didn't move. "It's only your cousin, Logan."

"No, he isn't only my cousin, he's got these three pint-sized assassins and they hate women! They'll burn her at the stake. And if they don't, Emmett will have her in front of a minister...I've got to get out there and save her!"

He was gone before the last word hit the air, with a shell-shocked Dane looking after him. Tess came to stand beside him, staring toward the closed door.

"Logan?" she asked.

He nodded.

"Where'd he go?"

"To San Antonio to save Kit from Emmett."

She turned and looked up at him. "I beg your pardon?"

"It seems that Emmett is in a perpetual state of readiness to marry the first available woman, but he can't get her past his three kids. Logan's gone to the rescue."

"I thought he wanted to find Tansy?"

"We did. She's staying with Emmett."

"And so is Kit, because she phoned last night with some story about being hijacked by white Indians and narrowly escaping being burned at the stake."

He smiled down at her. After a minute, he bent and kissed her with slow, lingering warmth. "I need a very strong cup of black coffee, and then you can tell me that again. Join me?"

She looped her arm through his. "I'd be delighted."

The thunderous knocking at the front door woke Kit, who'd overslept from sheer exhaustion. She and Tansy and Emmett had been up very late. Emmett had serenaded her. His voice grated like a nail file, but he did play the guitar quite well and she enjoyed listening to him. Then they talked about rodeo—which was the passion of his life—and about his plans for the future. They didn't talk a lot about the kids, who were carefully concealed behind curtains and under chairs listening. They'd been told three times to go to bed, but they never paid any attention to their father. Anyway, they were bent on finding out everyone's opinion of them.

The knocking stopped, but it was followed by a familiar bellow.

"Where is she?" Logan demanded.

"What a hell of a nerve, practically breaking into my house at this ungodly hour!" Emmett muttered. "Quiet down or I'll turn those kids loose on you!"

"Oh, God, not that, anything but that!" Logan groaned.

There were muffled giggles down the hall.

"Anyway, Tansy's asleep. Or she was, until you tried to knock the house down around our ears."

"I'm not looking for Tansy. Where's Kit?"

Kit's heart leaped in her chest. She couldn't believe that he'd come all this way for her! Had he seen Tess Lassiter and become concerned when he knew she was out here with the volatile San Antonio Deverells? Had he missed her?

She sat up in bed, just in time for Logan to throw open the door and confront her. She was dressed in the concealing flannel gown Tansy had loaned her.

"So there you are!" he growled.

"My, what a pretty picture." Emmett sighed as he saw her. "Darlin', you would look lovely propped up in my bed like that..."

"Out!" Logan shoved his cousin unceremoniously out the door and slammed it. "You lecher! She's only a child!"

"I'm going to marry her..." came through the door.

"Over my dead and decaying corpse!"

There was a muttering sound, like gagging, and quickly retreating footsteps.

"So much for him," Logan said with satisfaction. He stared at Kit for a long moment. "You can't marry him. It isn't love. He just likes women. There are so few who can get past those kids, he'll gladly latch on to anyone they like."

"I'm not blind," she said primly, folding her slender hands in her lap. "Why are you here? I thought you wanted me to find Tansy. I did."

"I know that. But you had no business moving in with the Family from Hell."

"What a way to talk about your own cousins!"

"Everybody knows about them. Nobody will even come near the place for fear of disappearing in the brush! Emmett lets those kids do anything they want to since his wife left. He doesn't care enough to make the barest attempt at control. He's too busy riding in rodeos to prove he's still a man, and getting his body broken to bits in the process! He can't get over the fact that his ex-wife left him."

Kit began to see the carefree Emmett in a new light, and he didn't seem quite so carefree anymore.

"Poor man," she said quietly.

"Poor man, the devil. He isn't your problem. Go home!"

Her eyebrows arched defiantly. "I don't work for you anymore. You can't tell me to walk to the corner!"

"No? Let me show you what I can get you to do, Miss Morris," he said, and started toward her.

Four

Kit froze. She'd never been alone in this kind of intimate setting with Logan, not even when she'd had to accompany him out of the country and they'd stayed in hotel suites together. Then, it had been all business and he'd never noticed her, no matter how she dressed or looked.

But now, the gown she was wearing might have been transparent as his dark eyes slid over the bodice and seemed to see right underneath it. He had a sophistication that was vaguely alarming. A woman's body was no mystery to him. She'd seen enough women come and go in his life in the past three years to know that he was experienced.

Her fingers grasped the cover and drew it up sharply to cover her breasts. She flushed as he paused by the bed and looked down at her.

Something changed in his face. He lifted one bushy eyebrow and deliberately let his eyes fall on her softly parted mouth.

He'd never wondered what it would feel like to taste Miss Morris's pert little mouth. But suddenly, he wanted the knowledge with a longing that corded his powerful body. Betsy was pushed to the back of his mind quite suddenly while he grappled with unbelievable desire for his ex-secretary.

"Will you please get out of here?" she squeaked.

He made an odd, hesitant movement and sat down on the bed beside her. His big hand, half the size of a dinner plate, folded around both of hers and detached them from their death grip on the coverlet.

"What are you afraid of?" he asked.

It was a tone he'd never used with her, a deep, husky pitch that was like warm velvet. She looked into his eyes closer than she'd ever seen them and became lost in their dark brown depths.

She wasn't breathing quite naturally. Neither was he, if the rise and fall of his broad chest under its charcoal-gray suit and white shirt was any indication. He smelled of some exotic cologne that appealed to her senses, and he was clean-shaven. The elegant Mr. Deverell was never disheveled or less than immaculate. Kit couldn't imagine him wearing jeans and chambray shirts as Emmett did.

"Answer me, Kit."

That was new, too—her name on his lips. It was always Morris this, Morris that. She searched his eyes helplessly. "I'm not afraid of you," she said absently.

Her vulnerability had a devastating effect on him. Their fights had become legend in the office building where he worked. Kit had a fiery temper and a stubborn nature, and he enjoyed the explosions that resulted from his prodding of both.

But she wasn't fighting now. She was sitting in his grasp like some exotic kitten, her big blue eyes wide and afraid and yet... almost welcoming. She had a beautiful complexion, he thought, and a mouth that looked as if it would feel like warm silk.

His body tautened with longing. He wasn't even thinking of consequences or other commitments as he captured her face in his big, warm hands and slowly bent to her upturned mouth.

She gasped as she felt his breath, coffee and mint scented, and the tentative brush of his mouth on her parted lips.

He felt her body jerk instinctively. His nose drew against her own. All he could see, think, breathe was the shape of her mouth under his. "I won't hurt you," he whispered, moving closer. "I can be gentle, even if I've never given you cause to believe it."

She felt his mouth touching hers, and it was like electricity. So many dreams, and here was the incredible, pulsing reality of his mouth against her own, his body so near that she could feel its heat and strength. She was floating, drowning.

She heard his breath catch, a tiny burst of sound that she knew was going to be a prelude to something volcanic and utterly destructive. And even as she yearned hopelessly for his touch, she knew that she couldn't give in to this madness. She didn't dare let him...!

She froze. "What about Betsy?" she said quickly.

His hands tightened on her head and his head lifted. His dazed eyes stared into hers. "What?"

"Don't forget Betsy!" she managed unsteadily, fighting his pull on her starved senses. "Remember Betsy, Mr. Deverell."

Mr. Deverell. He was Kit's boss and Betsy's would-be lover. He wondered how he could have forgotten that. His heavy brows met as his head lifted and Kit's pale face suddenly came into stark focus and he regained his lost wits.

Abruptly he let her go and stood up, turning his back while he struggled with unfamiliar feelings. He could feel his heart beating against his ribs, feel the tautness of his body with what he recognized dimly was desire. What was wrong with him? He didn't want Kit! He'd fired her. Betsy was warm and soft and loving, and her body promised heaven if he could ever maneuver her into bed. Kit was young and untried, very probably she'd never slept with anyone. God! he thought, and his body reacted sharply to the thought.

Kit pulled the covers back over her and averted her face. "I'd like to get dressed, if you don't mind," she said hesitantly.

"What? Oh. Certainly." He went out the door without a protest, and Kit thanked God for small miracles.

She couldn't quite believe what had almost happened. She had to be very careful from now on. Logan had made his opinion of Betsy quite clear, along with his commitment to the woman. Why he'd tried to kiss her, she couldn't comprehend. All she knew was that she mustn't, for her own sake, ever let him get close enough to try again.

Unrequited love was something she'd lived with for three long years. She knew Betsy and she didn't want Logan to fall victim to the woman, but there had to be another way to stop it. She really couldn't allow herself to become embroiled in a hopeless affair with him, even to save him from financial ruin. She'd certainly lose him that way. And when he'd had his fill of Kit's inexperience, probably Betsy's sophistication would snare him for sure. The thought was depressing, but it had to be faced. She couldn't let herself dream about him anymore. She had to get used to being without him in her life, in any capacity.

She got dressed in jeans and a sweatshirt, and went to the dining room where the rest of the family, Logan included, was sitting down to an enormous breakfast.

"Can he cook, or can't he?" Tansy enthused over the biscuits. "Emmett, you've missed your real vocation. God meant you to be a chef."

"I'd get dishpan hands." He chuckled. He glared at Logan. "That was a low blow, what you did in the hall."

Logan didn't look up from his scrambled eggs. "Yes, it was. I'll kill myself if you like."

Emmett didn't believe he'd heard that from his staid cousin, so he ignored it.

Kit didn't. Logan didn't sound like himself. She stared at him until he lifted his head, and what she saw in his eyes then made her blush furiously and look away.

Logan felt his fingers tremble on his fork. Damn it, what was *happening* to him? Only this morning, he'd been in complete control of his life. Or had he? He hadn't phoned Betsy to say he was leaving for San Antonio, or offered to bring her with him. He hadn't even phoned the office to tell them where he was. Chris would be dragged in to sub for him, which would make his brother furious. And why had he come dashing out here in the first place? To save Kit from Emmett.

That threat, at least, certainly seemed real enough. Emmett stared at her dreamily and kept making veiled references to how well he could provide for a new wife. The kids wanted to take her hunting with them, he added, which was a real honor.

"No, thanks." She chuckled. "I'd look sad with arrows sticking out all over me."

"Oh, none of that," Emmett protested. "They hunt with those electronic spotting guns. Toys, you know. I wouldn't dream of turning them loose with real bullets!"

"Did you know that if you get close enough with a radio signal you can ignite a dynamite cap?" Polk asked conversationally, which caused his father to choke on his biscuit.

"Out!" Tansy told the three, who had finished eating, while she hit Emmett on the back to dislodge the biscuit.

"I didn't say we'd ever done it," Polk muttered defensively. "Anyway, we couldn't get the man to sell us any dynamite."

"Oh, my *God!*" Emmett wailed.

"Wouldn't you like to enlist them in the Marine Corps?" Logan suggested. "You could lie about their ages."

"You won't feel like that when you have kids of your own," came the droll reply. "Flesh of your flesh, blood of your blood..."

"Speaking of blood, they're after the cat again," Tansy remarked.

Emmett muttered something violent and went to yell out the window. When he came back, he looked even older.

"I can't stand it. Please, for God's sake, marry me!" he pleaded with Kit, dropping to his knees by her chair and draping one long, muscular arm over her lap. "I'll reform. I'll stay home and cook barbecued ribs and breakfast and manage old man Regan's ranch. *Anything.* Just save me from those kids!"

Kit doubled over laughing. She just shook her head. "Thank you for the offer, but I really can't. I have to find missing people."

He looked up at her thoughtfully, his lips pursed, one eye narrowed. "Find people, do you? Okay. How are you at the reverse? Couldn't you hide me where those *kids* can't find me?"

"Why, you craven coward," Tansy chided. "Get off your knees and act like a proper father."

"I did try, Tansy," he said good-naturedly as he got gracefully to his feet. "But just as I broke the switch, one yelled to distract me, the second one positioned himself behind my knees and the third one knocked me over the second one into the river. I haven't really tried to hit one of them since."

"You don't have to hit them," Tansy continued, unabashed. "You could discipline them in other ways. Take away their television privileges."

He stared at her. "We don't have a television. Those kids threw a bowling ball through it. Thank God we have a good volunteer fire department here."

"Emmett, you're not the man I remember," Logan said, shaking his head.

"I'm not sure I ever was. Things have gone from bad to worse since she left me," he said, obviously referring to his ex-wife. "Since I got custody, no sane woman will have me. Maybe I could lock the kids up until I got one to the altar. Too late for you, of course," he said with a wistful smile in Kit's direction. "It's got to be a woman who doesn't know they exist until we're legally married!"

"Buffaloed by three children," Logan scoffed. "Imagine that."

"You try dealing with them," Emmett dared.

"Not me. I'm on the first plane to Houston this afternoon."

Emmett put down his coffee cup. "Why not stay until tomorrow?"

"Yes, why not?" Tansy seconded. "You and I get no time together these days, Logan. You're either too busy making money or traveling around the world or escorting that taffy-brained woman friend of yours around town."

He glared at her. "Let's leave Betsy out of this, shall we?"

"Suit yourself," Tansy replied. "You could fly back tomorrow with me. I can't stay around much longer. I'm only filling in for the housekeeper."

"My housekeeper," Emmett said. "The only woman west of the Pecos who isn't terrified of those kids."

"She had to have some minor surgery, but she'll be back tomorrow. Come on, son," Tansy coaxed. "You could use a day off. Besides, it's too late to go home and try to get anything done."

He didn't want to admit how much he wanted to stay. The way he felt about Kit was changing by the minute. He didn't want to leave her.

"You stay, too, Kit," Tansy commanded. "It's too late for you to go now, anyway."

"But I have my ticket . . ."

"You can use it tomorrow," Emmett coaxed, smiling at her. "I'll take you to a concert. Our local symphony has several this time of year. How do you fancy Aaron Copland?"

"Fanfare for the Common Man!" Kit said enthusiastically. "Oh, I'd love to go and hear some of his music!"

Logan was mildly surprised. The topic of music in any personal way hadn't come up since Kit had started working for him three years ago. He had no idea she liked Copland. So did he.

"How about Stravinsky?" he asked. "His work is largely of an experimental nature. A lot of people don't care for it."

"I like it," Kit said.

"So do I," Emmett seconded. "I think *The Firebird* is a tribute to his ability as a composer." He hesitated. "Let me make a couple of telephone calls. There's a special charity concert being given by a visiting orchestra, and I think they might include Stravinsky in their program. Let me find out."

He came back shaking his head. "Wrong night, I'm afraid," he said ruefully. "But there's a Mexican folk group in the city. Want to go see a Mexican ballet?"

"What about the children?" Kit asked.

"They like concerts and music of any sort," Emmett said. "They'll sit like mice. You wouldn't recognize them properly dressed and behaved."

"*I* certainly wouldn't." Tansy sniffed.

"That's because they used my flexible ropes to tie her to the bed the first night she got here," Emmett explained. "She taught them some new adjectives."

"You, too," Tansy chuckled. Her eyes twinkled. "It's so alive here, Kit. You really ought to marry Emmett. You'd never be bored."

"Not until the kids got grown, at least," he added. "Be a sport. Two little words—I do."

"I'm not that much of a sport, thanks just the same." She laughed. "I don't want to get married for years yet."

"It's a shame to wait for something that may never happen," Tansy said gently.

Kit's eyes were eloquent as she begged Tansy not to give away to Logan how she felt.

"All right," the elderly woman said, laughing softly. "I'll quit playing matchmaker. I would like to point out, though, that I have a perfectly marriage-able son who thinks you're wonderful..."

"I have never said...!" Logan began fiercely, color burning along his high cheekbones.

"Chris, my dear, *Chris,* not you," Tansy scoffed. "You've already announced to all and sundry that you can't wait to talk the beauteous Betsy into letting you support her for life in the manner to which she'd like to become accustomed."

"Betsy has money of her own," Logan said shortly.

"Indeed she does," Kit said, burning inside at the injustice of it.

"If you have something to say, Morris, spit it out," Logan challenged.

"Very well, I will." She threw down her napkin and got to her feet. "Your beautiful blond spider caused my nice old neighbor to kill himself over a stupid lottery ticket. He killed himself because she played him for a fool and got him to sign over every penny he had to her! That's why she's got money, Mr. Deverell. That's how she'll get yours, too," she added huskily. "She'll wind you around her little finger and promise you that lovely body. But you won't get it until she's got your name on a legal document of some sort. And then you still won't get it. But she'll have you. Drawn and quartered and bled to death, she'll have you."

She turned and left the room. The closed expression on Logan's broad, dark face had told her that he wasn't buying a word of it.

You simply couldn't talk to a stone wall.

* * *

Emmett caught up with her outside a few minutes later. He was smoking a cigarette and looking all around.

"It looks safe enough right here," he said, shoving his free hand into his jeans pocket. Under the wide brim of his hat, he was smiling as he joined her in the middle of the path that led into the distant pastures. The cool, dull brown horizon stretched out forever, a reminder that winter was almost here. "I have to pick times and places to smoke," he added ruefully. "Those kids have radar and smoke detectors and water guns in every shape and size. I guess they're right. I really should quit."

"It doesn't do your lungs much good, I suppose," she said.

"Mine or anyone else's. I don't smoke in closed rooms. It's too dangerous for bystanders." He flicked off an ash. "Funny, you know, the Indians used tobacco for hundreds of years, but they used it mostly for ceremonial purposes. Same thing with peyote. Mostly those substances weren't abused because they considered it sacrilege. Our culture abuses damned near everything."

"Especially natural resources." She turned and looked up at him. He seemed different when he wasn't pretending to be something he really wasn't. He looked somber and quiet and very, very masculine. If it hadn't been for the way she felt about Logan, she could have found herself falling all over this man.

"Did I put my nose on upside down again?" he asked with a cynically cocked eyebrow.

She laughed. "No. I was just thinking that you're many-faceted. I don't think I've seen the real you yet."

He shrugged. "Most people are pretty complex." He studied her face for a long moment. "You're without guile, aren't you? You have an honest, open face. I'll bet you return quarters you find on restaurant floors and obey parking signs and never tell lies."

"I try not to," she corrected. "I was raised not to cheat."

Her face closed up as she got the words out, and he saw her reaction.

"You tense when you get close to the subject of your parents."

"Do I? How big is this ranch?"

He hesitated, but only for a minute. He smiled and proceeded to describe the size and operation of the ranch for her, until a perplexed and irritated Logan came out to join them. He'd made all the necessary telephone calls, and he was still seething at Betsy's spitting fury because he hadn't phoned her sooner. He didn't like aggressive, snarling women. He respected intelligence, but Betsy had displayed cold, icy self-interest. Even through his physical infatuation for the woman, he recognized that.

"Do you know where the children are?" Kit asked suddenly. "Should I go look for them?"

"You'll find them in the barn with the new kittens," Emmett said. "That's where they usually are these days. Pretty little things, all different colors and all with long fur and blue eyes. Old Walt wanted to get rid of them, but we've got mice in the barn, so I figured they might as well stay."

He had a warmth about him that probably drew women like flies, Kit thought. She'd never had warmth from Logan, not even the two or three times she'd had flu or a virus since she'd worked for him. It was never "poor Kit." Rather, it was "when the hell are you coming back?"

"I'll go with you to look for them," Logan said, smoothly interposing himself between Kit and Emmett. "Sorry you're too busy to come with us," he said with a smile at his cousin. "But I know how it is."

"Not yet, you don't," Emmett said enigmatically, with a gleam in his eyes. "But you'll find out. How about that ballet?" he asked.

Kit hesitated. "I really don't feel quite up to it, but thanks anyway. Maybe Tansy and Logan . . . ?"

"Not me," Logan replied.

"Oh, well, maybe next trip," Emmett said. He winked at Kit. "If you married me, we could go to all sorts of cultural events."

"Right now, we're going to look at kittens and kids, thanks," Logan told him, taking Kit's arm. "Come along."

"Okay, I get the picture," Emmett said. He tipped his hat at Kit and strode away, whistling.

"I don't want to go anywhere with you," Kit snarled at Logan.

He let go of her arm and linked his big hands behind him to study her. He was wearing a long-sleeved white shirt and tie with his dark gray suit slacks. The shirtsleeves were rolled up to the elbow and he was wearing boots instead of street shoes. His dark, thick black hair was windblown and it gave his broad face an untamed appearance. Against the sky, he looked as if he were part of the history of the place.

"Who were your ancestors?" she asked unexpectedly.

"One of them was a lieutenant under Santa Ana," he mused, smiling at her shock. "You did know that the enemy troops sometimes raped and pillaged in the local communities? One of my ancestors was unfortunate enough to be in a house alone when they marched through. Along with the Mexican blood, I've got some very upper crust French and British."

It was a reminder that his background was much more monied than her own. She averted her eyes as they walked. "You're very dark."

"Most of that is from the sun. I spend a lot of time in the Mediterranean."

"Yes, I know."

He followed her toward the barn. It was warm for a November day. She pulled off her sweater and left her arms bare in the long-sleeved white shirt she was wearing with off-white jeans and boots.

"You look pretty western today," he remarked. "Didn't you live on a ranch once?"

She winced. "A long time ago. Look, there are the children . . . !"

He caught her arm and swung her back to face him.

"Your parents divorced, didn't they?" he said quietly.

He knew. She'd never been quite sure where he found out, or who had told him. She did know that her job required a thorough background check, and that he'd had one done before Dane's detective agency even opened for business.

Whoever had searched around in her record had certainly hit pay dirt. She didn't even bother to deny it. His eyes told her there was no point.

"It was a very messy divorce," she said averting her eyes. "They were arguing all the time. I don't like to remember those days. They both remarried after the divorce, but they only had a few years with their new spouses. Both my parents are dead now."

He pulled her into his big arms. She was warm and soft and vulnerable, and he loved the feeling it gave him to comfort her. That should have warned him that his emotions were teetering on the edge, but it didn't.

"Here, now," he muttered. He drew out a handkerchief and dabbed at her red, wet eyes with it. "Blow."

She did, hiccuping at the same time. "I never cry."

"I know. Not even when I yell."

He wiped the rest of her face and pressed the handkerchief into her hand. "Keep it. I've got dozens. Tansy has them hidden in every other drawer in my house. She thinks a man should have an endless supply."

"Why do you always call her Tansy instead of Mother?" she asked curiously.

"She doesn't seem old enough to be my mother at times," he replied with a wistful smile. "She's unique. Not that she doesn't worry me out of my damned mind just by being unique."

"Not every woman her age would try sailboarding."

"This is true." He pushed back the disheveled hair from her eyebrows. "You have skin like milk, Kit," he said, sketching her cheekbones. "It's almost transparent."

She flushed. "My mother...my mother had skin like that."

"Did she? Your people were ranchers, weren't they?"

"Yes. From over around El Paso," she said wearily. "Poor farmers. I come from a long line of poor people."

"Wealth or the lack of it never made character, Kit," he replied.

"It opens and closes doors, though."

He didn't argue. "I know the memories won't ever fade completely," he said. "But surely you're doing yourself no favors by burying them so deeply."

"It seemed best."

"I suppose so. Feel better now?"

"Yes. Thank you, Mr. Deverell."

He sighed. "Kit, after three years, don't you think you could manage to call me Logan?"

She searched his dark eyes in a long silence.

"Surely we know each other well enough," he persisted. He touched her lower lip, startled by its softness, its warmth and fullness. He couldn't seem to drag his eyes away from it. As he watched, her lips parted and his breath lingered in the very back of his throat.

His blood began to pound in his veins. His hands settled on her waist and drew her to him. There was nothing in his eyes except her mouth and even as he bent toward it, he knew he was going to regret this for the rest of his life.

"There's Betsy," she croaked defensively, pressing her hands flat against his broad, hard chest.

"Damn Betsy," he bit off against her soft mouth.

Five

Kit froze, but only for an instant. The reality of Logan's hard, expert mouth on her lips was all of heaven. She closed her eyes and felt as if her body was on fire from head to toe. He knew what to do with a woman's mouth, she thought dizzily, pressing closer. He knew *exactly* what to do!

Years of anguished longing, and it was happening. It was actually happening! These were Logan's arms enveloping her, this was Logan's mouth grinding so hungrily against her own.

She knew she'd live on this memory for the rest of her life. Her body lifted closer to his, and she moaned. The pressure of his mouth lessened and he began to tease and softly probe her lips, breaking through any defenses she might have had left, demanding surrender.

She gave it willingly. Her mouth opened to his penetration. She leaned into his big, powerful body and let him bring her so close that she could feel the corded muscles of his thighs, the flatness of his belly, the warmth of his broad chest against her soft breasts as his arms tightened.

He groaned and she answered him, her body so perfectly attuned to his that she matched every single movement he made.

Slowly her arms inched around his waist and she moved helplessly against the muscles of his body. He was against her, around her, sheltering and comforting her. Nothing could ever harm her again.

His tongue teased lightly into her mouth and then began quite suddenly to stab at it, producing the most intensely private sensations in the lower part of her body.

She tensed and tried to pull away, but his arms refused to release her. The movements became quicker, rhythmic, deep. She made a sound that she'd never made before and tried to twist upward in his arms, seeking blindly for a contact that would ease the powerful need he was building in her untried body.

As if he knew what she needed, his hands suddenly dropped to her hips and lifted her into the cradle of his own, bringing her into a contact that shocked even as it aroused.

She protested under his mouth. He lifted his head and watched her eyes with sensual mastery as his hands contracted, pressing her belly into a most blatant evidence of capability.

Her eyes shared everything with him: her fear, her vulnerability, her shock, her delight in his masculinity. Everything.

"Yes," he whispered gruffly. He nodded and his mouth settled slowly back on her own. She was no longer protesting anything, and his hands were moving her in a lazy rhythm, which produced choked little cries of pleasure.

When the building tension was more than she could bear, he wrapped his arms around her and all but crushed her, groaning into her mouth as he felt her shiver.

He was breathing raggedly and his legs were unsteady, as was her whole, soft body. He wanted her. There was a barn nearby, but it was full of kids. There was a house behind them, but it was full of adults. The ground was hard and cold, and very public. He cursed under his breath in anguish and his big body shuddered in response to her need.

He drew back, his face hard with passion and frustration.

Kit looked up at him, blazing with needs she hadn't even known existed. Her legs almost went out from under her, her body throbbed so with unsatisfied desire. "I hate you!" she said, choking. She hit his chest, hard, once, twice, shaking with what she supposed was rage at his presumption and his teasing.

"Here, it's all right," he whispered. His arms enveloped her, leaving a little space between their bodies as he comforted her, stroked her hair and whispered words of soft reassurance.

Tears ran down her cheeks as she struggled for composure. He felt a tremor in his own body. It had been a near thing. Imagine, he thought, with Kit, of all people!

His eyes opened and he saw the barn. The doors were closed, thank God, although there was one kid in the loft getting an eyeful. Polk. The quiet one. He darted back when he saw Logan's head lift.

"Spying on us, the devils," he murmured against Kit's temple.

"What?" Her soft voice was shaken, beautiful.

He lifted his head and smiled down at her. "The kids. They're up in the loft watching us."

She blushed. "Oh, my!"

His eyes kindled as he studied her. She was vulnerable. Now he knew it, but he didn't know what to do about it. His whole body ached from the heat of hers.

"You dress like someone who was raised in a convent," he said quietly. "But you kiss like a wild woman."

"Now you know what kind of night school courses I took year before last!" she said sarcastically, pushing at his chest.

He let her go, watching her try to get herself together. It amazed him that he could knock the logical, very prim Miss Morris off her pins. It delighted him. Betsy was a woman of the world, but this unique little sparrow wasn't used to men at all. The contrast was surprising. He found that he much preferred teaching Kit to having Betsy tutor him in what pleased her.

"Innocence in these confused times is a rare jewel indeed," he murmured, watching her.

She glared at him. "My jewel is none of your business," she muttered. "And how do you *know*, anyway?"

"I don't," he agreed. He grinned slowly. "But I could find out in ten minutes flat with a little cooperation," he added. "How about it?"

She latched on to what he was suggesting at once. "Mr. Deverell!"

She didn't know whether to gasp or laugh or kick him very hard. She walked on toward the barn without saying anything at all.

The barn door opened and all three kids smiled at them with very knowing faces.

"Where are the kittens?" Kit asked.

"Right over here," Amy volunteered, leading them. "Uh, Polk and Guy and I have to go get cleaned up. We'll see you later!"

There was a scurrying sound and the barn door closed, but Kit would have bet her socks that the kids were still inside.

She exchanged a glance with Logan, who actually grinned.

"Aren't they cute?" she asked, reaching down to pick up a kitten and stroke and caress it.

"Yes, they're cute," he mused, paying much more attention to Kit's rapt face than the small felines. He knelt beside her and gave the cats equal attention.

Nothing else was said for several long minutes.

"Damn!" came a long-suffering exclamation from Guy, who stood up along with his siblings, cast a disgusted look at the adults and stalked out of the barn. The other two went with him, trying to look both sheepish and angry at the same time.

Logan chuckled. "I suppose they were expecting a floor show."

"Those kids know too much already," she said, refusing to be baited. "But they're sweet children."

"They are not! Why do you think the family avoids this place like the plague? My cousin Belinda came down here to spend the night last year and the little monsters put an armadillo in the bed with her."

She whistled. "I'm glad they like me!"

"You'd better be. They defanged a rattler and shoved it in my room the first time I was fool enough to spend a night here."

"What did you do?"

"I went out the window, of course," he said. "Stark naked, because that's how I sleep, and I think I took at least two-hundred dollars worth of pane glass with me."

She could almost picture it. "Weren't you hurt?"

"Only my pride. The glass did very little damage. Fortunately for them. I haven't been back since, until now." He cocked an eyebrow at her. "But they'll be nice to me this time. They think I'm going to kiss you, and they can catch us at it and we'll be embarrassed."

"That's not a nice thing to say!"

"Why do you think they were hiding in here?" he asked patiently and smiled at her confusion. "Well, hide your head in the sand. But they're getting old enough to be curious, you know, and I'll bet Emmett hasn't told them zilch."

"He has so!" Amy interjected until two small hands, one on each side, clapped over her mouth.

"You varmints!" Logan raged at them. They'd eased back in and were crouched just inside the door behind a wall. "You'll swing for this, you sidewinders!"

"You'll have to catch us first, and you're old!" Guy called. The three of them escaped at a dead run.

"They're right," Kit said thoughtfully, eyeing him. "You *are* old. Thirty-five just this year."

He glared at her. "How would you like to be flattened out on the hay here for a few minutes?" he asked, glancing around. "The kids could sell tickets."

She cleared her throat. "I take it all back. You're young. You're in your prime, in fact."

"I was in my prime at eighteen, actually," he remarked. He smiled wickedly. "But I can still go all night."

She leaped up in the wake of outraged embarrassment, brushed off her jeans and stalked out the door just in time to connect with three small, warm bodies.

They all went sprawling, Kit included.

"I told you they were both too old," Guy muttered as he helped his siblings to their feet. "You have to watch teenagers to find out that sort of thing, not old people. Come on. We'll go down to the river and spy on Josh Landers and Cindy Gail when they get through fishing!"

Flushed with glee they rushed off again, leaving Kit muddled and out of sorts.

"I told you," Logan said from behind.

Emmett passed the kids, whirling around as they went by him like cyclones. He didn't ask where they were going. He wandered on down to join Kit and Logan.

"Why are you sitting on the ground?" Emmett asked Kit conversationally. "Is there a sudden chair shortage?"

"I'm just where your offspring left me, flat in the dirt," Kit told him. "They were down here spying on us—" She broke off when she realized what she was saying.

Emmett lifted an eyebrow and looked at Logan, who had a disgustingly smug and triumphant look on his face. "Oh," Emmett said. He smiled a little sadly, managing with one word to convey total understanding of the situation and regret on his own account.

"They're just curious," Emmett added after a minute, rocking back on his heels. "I told them the basics, and how to stay out of bad trouble with it all. They cleared their throats and pretended not to listen." He chuckled.

"Well, they were on their way down to the river. Something about a couple of teenagers fishing there..." Kit told him.

"Ohmigod!"

Emmett did an about-face and rushed off in the general direction the kids had taken.

"No wonder he's so slender and fit," Kit remarked, watching his figure slowly grow smaller in the distance. "I don't think I've seen him sit for five straight minutes since I've been here."

"The kids keep him on his toes. When he's here."

"Rodeo is very dangerous, isn't it?"

He nodded. "And for him more than most. His father died in a bull riding competition, right in the ring."

"How terrible for him!"

"That's not all of it. His mother killed herself soon after the funeral. That was when Emmett got married." He said it pointedly.

"He was lonely and grieving, wasn't he?" she asked.

"And determined to have a family so that he could fill up the house and banish the bad memories as quickly as possible. But the woman he married didn't take to motherhood, and she was really too young to settle down. She fell head over heels in love with a pretty ordinary man who'd worshiped her since high school. Emmett was never at home back then. He was paying off the mortgage on his father's land and just getting started good on the rodeo circuit. She should have stayed around. One of our more well-to-do relatives died last year and left Emmett fixed for life. I think Emmett's ex-wife married too young and wasn't really in love with Emmett."

"Then he doesn't have to do rodeo," she said.

"Not financially," he told her.

"Oh. I see." And she did. Emmett was harboring a wealth of hurt. Perhaps the pain and danger of rodeo made it go away for a while, or brought him close to memories of happier times when his father was alive. "But it can't be good for his kids."

"Maybe he does it to escape them," he murmured dryly.

"But they adore him. You can tell that they do, and it's mutual. But..."

"But he's afraid to get too close." Logan looked down at her with sudden comprehension. "He's afraid to love, because he's afraid of being left alone again. One way or another, he's lost every single person he ever loved."

Kit didn't reply. She kept walking and so did Logan, but the thought lodged in his mind and wouldn't be coaxed out. Was he that way, afraid to love? Betsy was temporary. Even as he'd admitted his physical need for her, there was never a time when he'd pictured her as a permanent part of his life. She hated cooking and housework and she and he never thought alike on the important issues. They argued often on politics and religion and just about everything else. The only real common ground they had was when Logan took her in his arms. But even that was superficial, shallow. There were times when he was almost certain that her enjoyment was nothing more than a facade.

Kit had said as much. She had to care about him, to be so protective. They'd been together a long time, he supposed, so maybe she felt a proprietary interest in his happiness. Still, she'd been upset enough to quit. Was she jealous?

He stuck his hands into his pockets as they walked, the big, husky man and the slender, graceful woman. It felt good to spend time with her. She didn't chatter or talk fashion and gossip at the expense of more serious subjects. Kit only spoke when she had something to say.

"Betsy was upset because I didn't bring her with me," he remarked.

She didn't look up. "You could ask her to fly out and meet you."

Logan gave Kit a calculated glance that she didn't see. "She'd want to sleep with me," he lied. "Emmett would go through the roof. He doesn't believe in that sort of thing."

She hated the very idea of Betsy in Logan's bed. Her hand clenched at her side, but she didn't make any remarks.

She didn't need to. The small movement didn't escape Logan's dark eyes. He smiled.

"Tansy's being very agreeable, don't you think?" she said, changing the subject.

"Yes. Suspicious, isn't it?" he added. "She probably didn't expect you to be this good at tracking her down." He stopped, and the look in his eyes was thoughtful. "In fact, it really was good detective work."

"I'm not just a typist, you know," she murmured. "I do have a brain and a few skills."

"If I never realized that, why would I go off and leave you in charge of the office for days at a time?" he asked. "I always recognized your talents, Kit."

Her heart jumped in her chest. "You never said you did."

"Why would I do a stupid thing like that?" he asked, amazed. "If I'd mentioned that you were being wasted in my office, you'd have quit and gone to work for a detective agency or something." He glowered at her. "As it happened, you did it anyway."

"After your beloved threw scalding coffee all over me and you took her side against me!"

"Of course I did, damn it!" He bit off the words. "I wasn't trying to get *you* into bed, was I?"

She went scarlet. Her palm itched to land against that massive jaw, but she restrained it—barely.

"You hopeless little prude," he said shortly, dark eyes blazing. "To you, like Emmett, sex is something that only happens between married people, I suppose?"

"Yes, it is. Or it should be," she said forcefully. "I suppose you think it's right that carelessness produces thousands of unwanted babies? Or that it's all right to sleep around indiscriminately and spread terrible diseases?"

He didn't reply immediately. "No," he said finally. "I don't think it's right. I believe in prevention and safety, and I practice them."

She didn't have a comeback for that. She started walking again.

"How's your secretarial staff?" she asked. "Are they coping with your absence?"

"Chris is having something of a problem with one of them."

"Which one?"

"Margo."

"The one with the cleavage who can spell."

He chuckled. "That's right. She likes rich men."

She bit her tongue to hold back a remark about another woman close to him who did, too.

"Don't hold back," he told her, smiling as if he knew what she was doing and thinking. He stretched lazily. "The chain-smoker has bronchitis, but she's still dragging in to work. The other one seems to be managing, too, now that you'd shown her where you hid all my most important files."

"I didn't hide them." She gritted her teeth. "I filed them."

"Only an idiot would file an oil account under *T* for Texas."

She glared at him. "It isn't *T* for Texas, it's *T* for Texas Premium Oil Company!"

"Well, I had the girls refile things so that I could find them. Oil accounts under Oil, tax accounts under Taxes and clients under the last names."

"Not under the company names?"

"It's none of your business anymore," he said smugly. "You quit."

"I did not! You fired me!"

He shrugged his broad shoulders. "We had those potted things moved out into the hall, too."

She gasped. "They'll die! They were by the window so that they could get sunlight! They can't live in the shade."

He frowned. "So that's why they're wilting."

"My poor plants!"

"There's probably still time to save them," he remarked casually. He glanced at her. "You could come back. I'd give you a raise."

"And stand by while darling Betsy practices her Napoleon impression."

"She is not tyrannical!"

"Ask Melody or Margo or Harriet," she shot back. "I dare you! She may be sweetness and light to you, but she's poison to everyone else—especially to her own sex! What she did to poor old Bill Kingsley she's going to do to you, and I'll be the last one crying when you're sleeping in a downtown mission!''

His chest rose and fell roughly with anger. Damn, she was a bossy woman! He had no intention of letting her lead him around, tell him whom to date, what to think!

''Betsy is *my* business,'' he said harshly. ''You're only jealous, because she's beautiful and you aren't!''

He'd never said that before, even if he'd always thought it. Kit was used to people looking through her. She knew she wasn't pretty. But that was hardly why she disliked Betsy.

She didn't fight back. It would have been admitting that he was right. She walked on, alone, her eyes sad and quiet.

Behind her, Logan slapped his fist angrily against his thigh. Damn his tongue! He'd been furious, but those hurtful words had really slipped out unconsciously.

It was pure cussedness, he knew, but he couldn't think of any way to take it back—and still save face. Kit went very quiet when she was hurt. It was the only time she didn't spit and claw. He remembered how she'd responded to him earlier, and how protective she was. She was probably in love with him, and he had more power to hurt her than anyone else on earth.

He watched her with a gnawing hunger. Love wasn't an easy thing to throw away. All the same, he was getting married and Kit was off-limits. He shouldn't have kissed her like that. She'd said that it was unfair to Betsy, and it was.

The problem was that Kit aroused him even more than Betsy did. He couldn't let that situation develop. He had principles, even if he was only just discovering them. He might as well let Kit think he had a low opinion of her looks. Perhaps it would spare her any more hurt at his hands if he could turn her infatuation to dislike. He was going to marry Betsy. All he had to do was keep that in mind, then perhaps he could stop having these inconvenient urges to seduce Kit.

But she didn't hate him. That was all too apparent when he stared at her across the supper table and her eyes fell in blushing confusion to her plate. His heart began to race in his chest as he realized how easily he could disconcert her. His eyes fell to her mouth. He remembered much too vividly how it felt to kiss her, to hold her. He'd tried for the rest of the day to put that sweet interlude out of his mind, but he couldn't. The more he thought about it, the more he wanted it again.

With an angry movement of his hand, he reached for his coffee cup and accidentally hit it, sloshing hot coffee right across the table onto Kit's white blouse.

She gasped, grabbing a napkin to dab at it. While Logan tried to apologize, she glared at him. "Been taking lessons from Betsy, have we?" she asked with cool sarcasm. "No need to worry, it will wash out. Excuse me, please."

She was grateful for the incident in a way, because it gave her the opportunity to escape. Everyone was looking at her. The kids were probably recalling every lurid minute they'd witnessed from the barn, and Emmett was speculative and a little sad. Tansy was hiding amusement. Logan—well, Logan was a puzzle altogether. But Kit had felt like a lab specimen. By the time she changed and went back downstairs, supper would be over and she could escape.

After she stripped off the blouse, she soaked it in the bathroom sink. Her flimsy bra was wet, too, from the coffee. That, she thought resignedly, would have to be washed as well. As she unfastened it, her elbow caught a bottle of shampoo and knocked it across into the bathtub with a heavy thump. The noise concealed a brief knock at the door, and her own movements, as she retrieved and replaced the shampoo, masked the sound of footsteps.

She slid her bra into the sink and was swirling it through the water when a soft sound beside her made her turn her head.

Logan was holding the door open, and he was making no pretense of not looking. His eyes, dark with surprise and fascination, slid over her breasts as if they belonged to him, savoring their firm, tip-tilted contours, enjoying their dusky hard tips and creamy texture.

He hadn't expected this when he'd come after her, albeit reluctantly, to apologize. Seeing her half nude had knocked every sane thought right out of his mind. He was enthralled by the utter beauty of her. He leaned against the door frame and gave his eyes free rein. "I don't think there's any work of art in the world that could compare favorably to a woman's bare breasts," he said quietly, and without offensive intent. "Yours are beautiful, Kit. Absolutely breathtaking."

They must have been, because she actually saw his breathing change. Her eyes fell and she saw something else change, too, before she quickly lifted her eyes again and quickly folded her arms over her breasts.

"I won't embarrass you any more than I have," he said softly. "It's all right. I only came after you to apologize. Spilling the coffee really was an accident."

"I knew that," she said. Her voice was husky and she felt her body ache with new sensations, new hungers. Her breasts began to swell and tingle and throb. His hands were like plates, she thought as she stared at him. They would cover her breasts completely. They would be warm and a little rough, and her body would tremble because it would feel so sweet to have them on her bare skin.

The feelings frightened her. She shivered, her eyes wide and a little apprehensive as she looked at him.

Logan saw her hunger and reacted to it. He wanted her. God, he wanted her! And if her vulnerability was any indication, she wanted him just as much.

"You've never known a man's eyes or hands before, have you, Kit?" he asked very gently.

She couldn't get a word past her tight throat. She shook her head.

His eyes traced her body with quiet, aching appreciation. He had to touch her. He couldn't help himself; he had to! "There is, as they say, a first time for everything, little one," he said.

He sounded almost solemn. And as she watched, he pushed away from the doorframe, walked slowly inside and closed and locked the door behind him.

Six

————

Kit couldn't find the right words to express what she felt. It would have been muddled if she had. She wanted him to look at her; she ached for him to touch her. But it was wrong, because he was only interested in the physical intimacy, and because he was going to marry Betsy. She should scream her head off and order him out of the room, and her brain wanted to, but her body trembled helplessly as he walked toward her. Her eyes told him that he could have anything he wanted.

His own eyes were stormy, not easily read at all. His broad face was without humor or teasing. It was as solemn as if he were in church.

Without a word, he reached and disengaged her hands from her breasts. He moved them away from her body and brought them to her sides. Then he looked at her, with awe and quiet delight while she struggled to breathe normally and failed.

When one big hand came up and gently touched just the tip of her breast, a weak cry escaped her throat.

"This is where you're most sensitive," he said, tracing the hard, erect tip. He watched her eyes while he touched it, savoring its heat and hardness with his fingers and then with his palm. "It frightens you to be vulnerable, doesn't it?"

"Yes," she whispered.

"Don't you think I am?" he asked surprisingly. His fingers went to the Western-cut shirt he was wearing and flicked open the pearly snaps.

Her eyes lit up with pure delight as she gazed at the thick dark hair on his broad, bronzed chest.

"Here. Touch me where I'm touching you."

He drew her fingers to his chest, and let her feel the hard tip over his heart.

She traced it and he caught his breath, laughing softly at her surprise.

"When men and women make love, there's no real master," he said, moving so that his big hand could completely cover her soft breast. "Both become vulnerable. Fragile..."

He bent and kissed her parted lips with a tenderness that was indescribable. His hands were gentle on her body, tracing, learning, exploring, until he knew every centimeter of skin above her waist.

Kit, too, was learning. Her hands buried themselves in that thick pelt and tugged at it with a pleasurable rhythm. But all too soon, it was no longer enough, and without conscious intent, she stepped even closer to him and relaxed completely against his aroused body.

"No," he whispered. His big hand dropped to her hip and gently moved her back. His mouth teased hers again. "This isn't the time or the place."

She looked up into his dark, patient eyes. "It makes me ache," she whispered, trying to put her feelings into words.

"Yes. Me, too." He drew his face against hers. Both hands slid over her breasts and gently caressed them. "You're like silk all over, aren't you?" he whispered. His mouth slid down her throat, over her shoulders and her collarbone. It eased down, down, until it suddenly opened on her soft breast. He touched it with his tongue, producing new and volatile hungers that arched Kit's body like a bow.

"Hold on, baby," he whispered roughly.

While she was trying dizzily to comprehend what he meant, his head lifted. For an instant, the coolness of the room was uncomfortable on the moist place he'd left on her skin. Then he burrowed against her, found the hard nipple, took it completely into his mouth and began to suckle it.

For a few seconds, Kit froze. Then she tautened until her muscles felt in danger of shattering. Her body arched and drew in and she pushed up against his mouth as if it were the source of life itself.

Her hands were in his thick, dark hair. They clung, trembling, as the fever he kindled burned high and bright. She shivered, and shivered again, and began to moan. He made a fierce sound and the suction grew harder, more insistent.

Something snapped in Kit's body. She shuddered as a wave of pleasure hit her right in the core of her body and convulsed her into utter satisfaction.

She couldn't stop trembling. Her legs were too weak to hold her up. Logan had lifted his head and was looking at her, but she was too busy trying to get her breath back and stop her heart from shaking her to bits to notice. Gently he pressed her bare breasts against his equally bare chest, starting up new sensations as she felt the sexy abrasiveness of his body hair against her warm skin.

He held her cheek there, and under his muscular chest she could hear the irregular beat of his heart as he smoothed her hair back, and brushed soft kisses against her temple.

She thought that she could never look him in the face again. Her abandon had embarrassed and sickened her.

She tried to pull away, finally, but he wouldn't let her. He tilted her shamed face up to his eyes and searched it quietly. It was somehow more profound because he didn't speak. His fingers touched her face, cherished it, while he examined every facet of her from the chin up as if he'd never looked at her before.

"I'm plain," she said in a brittle tone. "You said so."

"You infuriate me at times. I say a lot of things I don't mean and you know it." His voice deepened. "You know me better than anyone else in the world does, except in one way. In the ultimate way."

Her cheeks burned with heat.

"I satisfied you, didn't I?" he asked, his voice soft and intimate. Her eyes fell and she couldn't speak. "Yes, I thought so. You're incredibly naive, Kit. You have no real comprehension of what sex is all about. Perhaps now you understand a little better how powerful a force attraction can be." He put a fist under her chin and tilted up her rebellious face. "I could have you right here, standing up," he said harshly. "And after the first five seconds, you'd be tearing the clothes away from our bodies for me. That's how much you want me."

"That's cruel," she choked.

"That's the truth." His hands framed her face. He bent and kissed her forcefully, roughly, and jerked his mouth away. "You'd walk to hell for me if I asked you to."

She stiffened in his embrace and her face turned deathly pale.

"This is why you left in the first place," he said huskily. "You had to get out because it was killing you to see me with Betsy! You love me!"

The truth of it was in her wide, wounded eyes, blue pools in the white oasis of her face. She looked at him as if he'd put a knife through her.

Until he'd said the words, he hadn't really known. But now he did, and suddenly the past three years fell into place. So much of his life was involved with Kit's. He'd fired her, but he hadn't really wanted her to leave. He'd missed her, ached for her company. Now he ached in another way, in a damned inconvenient way, and he'd just crossed the barrier between friendship and sex. And he'd compounded the error by doing it with a woman who was madly in love with him.

"I never used to be cruel," he said almost to himself. He winced as he searched her face. "Everything I say makes it worse, doesn't it?"

"Would you hand me a towel, please?" she asked dully.

"Of course." He turned away and removed one from the rack to give her. She wrapped it around her like a blanket and stood there, defeated, humiliated, drained.

"If you could make some excuse for me," she said, her voice so low that he had to strain to hear it. "A headache?"

"I can do that."

Her eyes closed, shutting him out. She wished she could go through the floor. What must he think of her now?

He drew her forehead to his chest and held it there, his expression troubled. "I'm sorry. I had no right to touch you like that."

She bit back tears. She didn't say a word, or yield an inch.

His teeth ground together as silvery waves of pleasure teased his body. Even the smell of her was enough to trigger it. "My God, I want to make love to you, Kit!" He choked.

She wanted it, too, but it was impossible. "You're engaged," she reminded him. "What happened ... wasn't right."

He sighed heavily. "Yes, you're obsessed with doing the right thing, aren't you? I used to be, too, until

Betsy came along and my glands all exploded. I'd been so busy making money and speculating on ways to make more that I'd all but given up women in the past six months, until Betsy walked in the door." He brushed his lips over her hair. "There you sat, waiting for me to wake up. But I turned the wrong way, didn't I?"

"You can't help loving someone."

She should know. But she was assuming he loved Betsy, and he didn't. He wanted her and the only way he could get her was to get married. Now, he wasn't sure that it actually was what he wanted anymore. He scowled as confused thoughts began to gnaw at him.

"Let me go, Logan," she said, tugging at his hands. "You'd better leave now."

He stared at her with undisguised longing. "If we were anywhere else, I'd ask you to come to bed with me. I could protect you, Kit. There'd be no risk at all."

She stared back, wavering. But there was Betsy, and sleeping with a man she wasn't married to was wrong. No. She couldn't do that. Her eyes fell.

"Even if that kind of thing is right for the whole rest of the world, it isn't right for me. I . . . I'm not made for one-night stands."

He watched her while he snapped his shirt buttons back up, his face taut and somber. "I don't think one night would be enough," he said. "You're starved for me, Kit. Not just hungry. Starved."

"I am not!" she said miserably, lifting wild blue eyes to his.

"If you're not," he replied quietly, "then explain to me how I managed to fulfill you just by putting my mouth to your breast. Or do you think it's a common occurrence for women?"

She felt her face go even whiter at the charge. "If you're implying that I'm wanton...!"

"Oh, yes, you're wanton," he said huskily. "Sexy as hell and heaven to kiss. I'd give my right arm to go all the way with you."

In that moment he looked as if he actually meant it. His posture was as intense as the way he was looking at her.

"You're engaged," she said sadly.

"Yes."

She felt cold. "I'm sure that... that Betsy attracts you just as much. And probably any experienced man could have made me feel the same as you just did."

"I wouldn't bet on it."

"Maybe I should ask Emmett..."

"I'll break your neck if I catch you so much as looking at Emmett!" he burst out, but returned to normal in a flash, his usual domineering, impatient, outrageous self.

"How interesting," she said calmly.

"You little fool, he's out of your league," he persisted, hating the very thought of her with his cousin.

"He wants to marry me. He said so."

Logan's lips compressed. He glared at her. "He can't have you."

She felt intimidated by the look he was giving her. He was bristling with bad temper, she thought, and felt an involuntary surge of compassion for him. He wasn't a bad man. He loved Betsy, that was all. Probably he was missing her, and Kit had been a stand-in. She felt sad, knowing that.

"Logan, you have your own life," she said gently. "Your own priorities. However I feel, and you don't really know," she emphasized, "Betsy should be your main concern right now."

His eyes narrowed in anger. "I can manage my own private life, thank you."

"Good. Why don't you go and do it?"

"I might as well," he said irritably. He gave her one long, lingering look, and found that he had to force his legs to move. She'd been so sweet in his arms. But she was right. He had Betsy to think about. Touching Kit had been in no way honorable, even if it had been heaven.

He finally started toward the door. He didn't say another word. He unlocked the door and didn't even bother to close it on his way out.

Much later, when Kit was in bed, Tansy came to check on her.

"Logan's outside howling at the moon," Tansy said. "He's utterly demolished half a glass of good Scotch whiskey. Your doing, I presume?"

"I, uh, we had a slight misunderstanding. He seems to feel that he can be engaged to Betsy and still make a grab for me if he feels like it," she said through her teeth, without elaborating on her own part in her downfall.

Tansy took one of Kit's hands gently in hers. "Let me tell you something you may not realize. In three years, you've been all Logan ever talked about when he came to see me. It was always Kit said this, Kit did that. You've been his world all that time.''

"Then why is he going to marry Betsy?"

Tansy let go of her hand and shrugged. "Who can fathom the mind of a man?" she asked. "I think perhaps he hasn't realized yet how much a part of him you are. Sometimes it takes a drastic change to make a man look a different way at something. I don't believe he's ever really seen you, Kit. How's that for irony?"

He'd seen her in ways she couldn't tell his mother, too. She didn't dare bare her soul that far. "If he marries that woman, he'll never recover," Kit said sadly. "But he won't listen. He just won't listen!"

"He's not going to admit that he made that kind of mistake, I'm afraid," Tansy said. "Logan never would admit to being in the wrong. Too, perhaps he resents having you try to nurture him. He likes to think that he's doing the nurturing. But Betsy is a bad woman, Kit," she added quietly. "A bad egg. I know the danger Logan is in. I just don't know what to do about it, short of having the kids kidnap Betsy." She frowned thoughtfully. "I wonder if I could get Emmett to bribe them...."

Kit laughed reluctantly at the thought of Betsy tied to a stake. "It's an idea."

"Kit, please don't give up on him," Tansy pleaded. "Chris and I are the love 'em and leave 'em type. But Logan is different. He's deep and when he loves, it's with everything he has, everything he is. A man like that who loves the wrong woman paves the way to his own destruction."

"Yes, I know," she said. "But if he loves her..."

"If he loved her, he wouldn't have been shut up in a bathroom with you for several minutes," Tansy said with a wicked grin.

"How...?"

"Those kids, how else?" Tansy sighed. "They were up here trying to take the doorknob off with a screwdriver when Emmett caught them. Don't worry." She chuckled at Kit's horror. "The walls are two inches thick, nothing gets past them. But if they'd managed to get the doorknob off, things would have gotten a bit interesting..."

Kit buried her face in her hands. "Oh, dear," she whispered, thinking how embarrassing it would have been, even though nothing terribly indiscreet had happened.

"Don't be like this, sweetheart," Tansy said gently. "My goodness, you do take life so seriously. How do you expect to live if you can't bend the rules occasionally? It isn't as if you're a promiscuous person who thrives on flaunting herself. You're a nice, decent woman, and I do wish it was you instead of Betsy that I was going to have for a daughter-in-law."

"Nothing really terrible went on in there," she began.

"So what if it had? Since when have you been perfect?" Tansy smiled. "My dear, you have a very rigid and rather unflattering view of God if you think He's as narrow-minded and petty as most human beings are. Give Him credit for knowing all about you, not just what shows."

"I thought you didn't go to church," Kit said, amazed.

"I don't. There are too many denominations fighting each other, when they should be trying to please God. Fellowship is nice, but I don't think just going to church alone will get a mean person into heaven."

"Maybe not," Kit said. "But without some kind of rules, what would we have?"

"What we've got," Tansy told her. "The most confused generation of kids who ever lived on the planet. There are no rules, no values, no heroes. Have you ever studied ancient civilizations, Kit?"

"Not really."

"The first sign of a declining civilization is a decline in the arts. And I think we have a very definite decline in culture and art. It's been replaced by video games and plastic toys and television and VCRs."

"I'm glad the kids don't have a video camera," Kit said with faint humor as she began to relax a little.

Tansy chuckled. "Remind me to give them one for Christmas."

"Poor Emmett! He'll never get a bride then!"

"Are you feeling better?" Tansy asked. "A little less tormented?"

"Yes. You're nice medicine."

"I've never been called that. Well, off to bed. We go back to Houston in the morning." Her eyes twinkled at Kit. "After that, who knows?"

"Tansy, you won't vanish again!"

"Dear girl, if I stay in one place very long, I'll die there. At my age, one must keep moving or freeze up. If old age catches me, it'll have to outrun me." She got up and went to the door. "I'd lock this," she said. "The kids don't have a VCR, but they do have a Polaroid camera . . ."

Kit leaped out of bed without an argument. She could imagine the kind of photographs she might appear in if she left that door unlocked, even though she didn't sleep naked.

At breakfast the next morning, the kids were gathered around and snickering faintly as they looked from a hung over, very quiet Logan to a shy Kit.

"I hid the screwdrivers, Kit, don't worry," Emmett said with a wicked glance toward her and then Logan. "You're safe this morning. All the same, I wouldn't lock myself in any more bathrooms with Logan around here, if I were you. They've got this Polaroid camera and a saw . . ."

"What screwdriver?" Logan asked with restrained shock.

"The one they were using to take the doorknob off Kit's bathroom door," Emmett said smoothly.

Logan put down his fork. "My God!" he exclaimed, staring at the children.

"He never tells us nothing!" Guy muttered, and when he scowled at Emmett, it was like looking at a miniature of the man.

"Emmett, have you ever considered giving up rodeo for a season and raising your kids?" Logan asked curtly.

Emmett glared at him. "They're my kids and it's my life. I don't come up to Houston and try to tell you how to live, do I?"

"Somebody ought to," Tansy remarked pleasantly, "before he ruins it."

"Thank you very much," Logan growled at his mother.

She smiled vacantly. "Why, you're welcome, dear. Emmett, wouldn't you like to bring the kids and come and visit Logan? I'd *love* for you to meet his new fiancée...!"

"I don't have spare bedrooms," Logan said abruptly.

"You do so," Tansy argued. "Three of them."

"They're being remodeled."

"They are not," she argued.

"They will be by tomorrow," he said under his breath. "Besides, Emmett's riding in a rodeo out in Montana."

"In the snow?" Tansy exclaimed.

"Arizona," Emmett corrected lazily. He glared at Logan. "Some cousin you are. I offer you the hospitality of my home and loving family, and you don't even want us to stay a night with you."

"Loving family?" Logan's eyes widened. He looked at the kids. "Them?"

"We're loving," Amy said, glaring at him.

"All of us," Guy seconded, scowling.

"You better not say we ain't loving, mister," Polk added.

"That's my kids," Emmett said smugly. "Listen up, you kids, how would you like Kit there for a mother?"

"She ain't pretty," Guy said.

"She's nice, though," Amy interrupted. "And she doesn't have to fix her face every two minutes and paint her fingernails like that lady in the glittery dress that you brought home that night you thought we were asleep," she reminded Emmett.

Polk frowned as Emmett's dark face flushed. "He sure took her away in a hurry when he saw us, didn't he?"

"Will you stop?" Emmett asked him.

Kit chuckled to herself. She did like Emmett. But not enough to marry him.

"You could marry that glittery lady," Polk suggested. "She said she sure did like your money. She didn't like us much, though. What was it she called us, Guy?"

"Guy, shut up!" Emmett raged.

"You were so married to our mama, weren't you, Emmett?" Amy asked. She called her father by his given name, a habit he'd reluctantly gotten used to because he couldn't seem to break it.

"Yes, I was, Amy," he said.

"So that means we're not—"

"*Amy,* I'm warning you!" Emmett threatened.

"Oh, very well, Emmett," she said primly, dabbing at her mouth. "May we be excused?"

"Why? Are you in a rush to hijack a truck or something?"

They glared at him. "We're helping Mrs. Gibbs bake a cake. She's the foreman's wife," Amy explained to everyone. "She said we could."

"God help Mrs. Gibbs."

"Some father you are," Logan muttered as the kids escaped out the backdoor, heading for the foreman's house.

"Mrs. Gibbs has nerves of steel and they listen to her," he argued.

"They ought to be listening to you," Logan persisted.

"Talk about soreheads!" Emmett said, making a clicking sound. "Frustration sure doesn't sit well with you, does it? And you ought to be ashamed of yourself, making advances to Kit when you're engaged to that Betsy woman. Something I would *never* do if you got engaged to me, Kit, my dear," he added silkily.

"Oh, for God's sake!" Logan roared. He threw down his napkin and walked out of the room.

His back was growing very familiar to Kit, who saw more of it lately than she ever had.

"I really can't marry you, Emmett. I'm sorry," Kit said.

"I'm persistent," he remarked with a lazy smile. "Don't say I didn't warn you."

She smiled, but it wasn't an encouraging smile.

Two hours later, they said their goodbyes and Logan drove Kit and Tansy to the airport. Their seats were widely separated, and for that small mercy Kit was glad. It was good to go home and get away from the enforced intimacy with Logan. He barely spoke to her now, and she was equally glad to avoid him. After the explosive interlude they'd shared, she didn't know how to behave with him. All she knew was that she didn't want to end up in his bed because he was frustrated and she was weak. Going back to Houston and keeping out of his way seemed the only sensible thing to do.

Logan was thinking the same thing. He'd just begun to realize what a horrible mistake he'd be making if he married Betsy. But admitting it was next to impossible. It would kill his pride.

On the other hand, Kit's well-meant interference had only made him dig his heels in deeper. All the way back home he did his best to convince himself that Kit was wrong and he was right about Betsy. But the doubts were beginning to outweigh the certainties in the relationship. He was at a crossroads and he honestly didn't know which way to turn.

Seven

————

Dane was fascinated by the report Kit gave him when she got back to the office.

"You're kidding," he remarked when she finished. "Nobody has children like that in real life. Are you sure you haven't been reading fiction?"

"Why don't you go out there and see for yourself?" she suggested dryly.

"No, thanks!" He shook his head. "What a family. Tansy went home with Logan, did she?"

"Yes, but nobody knows how long she'll stay. When Betsy walks through the door, I expect Tansy will vanish again," she said dejectedly.

"That means more business for us." Dane chuckled.

"I suppose."

* * *

Dane gave Kit a new case to work on, tracking down a bail jumper this time. But the man wasn't a dangerous criminal; he was a forger who'd made "bush bond."

With a little help from the skip-tracing department, specifically from Doris, Kit latched on to an address downtown in the red-light district. There was only one way to get close to that address, and she didn't find it at all amusing.

The sacrifices I make for this job, she thought as she adjusted her skin-tight, green sequined miniskirt and black halter with matching black silk hose. She overapplied her makeup and saturated herself in sweet perfume. Then she drove to the address and started to walk, rather self-consciously, along the crowded sidewalk between two adult bookstores.

"Hey, who are you? This is my spot! What do you think you're doing, girl?"

The questioner was the real thing, with bleached blond hair and good skin, of which most was on blatant display.

Kit glanced around nervously and moved closer to the blonde. "I'm a detective," she whispered. "I'm trying to find a bail jumper. Please don't give me away."

The woman looked impressed. She pursed her lips and nodded. "A detective? For real?"

"I'm afraid so." She eyed the other woman curiously. "I saw *Pretty Woman.* You aren't...?"

Delighted laughter met her query. "No. But I wouldn't mind meeting somebody with an expensive car who brought me flowers. Now in this job, that's *real* fantasy!" She and Kit both laughed.

"Who's this dude you're looking for?" the woman asked, glancing around. "Maybe I know him."

"This is a copy of his driver's license photo," Kit said, producing it. She didn't mention how she'd managed to obtain it, and the hooker didn't ask.

"I've seen him!" the woman said. "He doesn't have much time for us, but he passes here every night on his way to that adults only video place at the corner. Matter of fact, he'll be along about nine, if he follows his usual routine."

Kit glanced at her watch. "Mind if I stick with you?" she asked, nervous now that she was attracting attention from men and pimps alike.

The hooker chuckled. "This isn't your scene at all, is it, honey?"

"Well, no."

The other woman smiled at Kit—really smiled at her. "You haven't looked down your nose at me once."

"I don't think any of us are so good that we can look down on anybody else," Kit replied with a shrug, then shivered a little in the cold. "How do you keep warm?"

"The street people have fires in barrels down the alley. We usually take a break and go stand down there. They don't mind us. Society's cast-offs stick together."

Kit felt a surge of sympathy for the woman, who looked to be in her thirties. But she had a worn-out look in her eyes. "Don't you worry about, well, about diseases?"

"All the time," she was told. "I had a friend who died of AIDS last month." She shook her head. "We're all careful now. *Real* careful."

"Why do you do this?"

"It's all I know how to do. Even this was better than home, when I was thirteen," she said with a haunted look in her eyes. She shivered a little, and suddenly looked so fragile and pathetic that Kit could have cried for her. "Well, would you look at that hunk?" she said suddenly, nodding toward an approaching crowd. "He sure isn't down here for a pickup, I'll bet."

Kit followed her gaze and caught her breath. No, she thought. No, I can't be seeing this.

But she was. It was Logan, breathing fire in a figurative sense. And not only did he see Kit, but he obviously knew she was here.

"Doris told me," he said without preamble. "Dane must be out of his mind to let you come down here alone at night! What's the matter with you, are you daft? Don't you know what kind of people these are?"

Kit was offended. She glared at him. "Yes, I know," she said. "But do you? Don't insult my friend!"

The hooker looked as shocked as Logan did.

"You could be out here if circumstances hadn't made you rich," Kit said. "Anyone could. Look around you! These people didn't wake up one morning and decide to wander around the back streets of the city!"

Logan hesitated. He glanced at the blonde, who was gaping at Kit.

"You know her, I guess?" the hooker asked.

"She works for me. At least, she did before I fired her."

"If you fired her, you're pretty stupid for a handsome, rich man," the hooker said, but she smiled. So did Logan.

"Hey, look, there he is!" the hooker said urgently, pointing to a small, dark man in a camouflage jacket.

"Glory be!"

Kit was running before the other two could say a word. When the man realized that he was being chased, he took off. Kit followed him. The high heels were hampering her. She stopped just long enough to strip them off and kept running, panting for breath as the small man dodged cars to cross the street, with Kit in hot pursuit.

"Stop!" she yelled after him.

He looked over his shoulder when she yelled and lost his footing. He went down with muttered curses, tripping other people on the way.

Kit ran to him, dragging out the handcuffs she'd brought from the office. She flipped him over, linked a cuff over one wrist, crossed it over the other and cuffed that one, too.

She laughed, her senses heightened with success, still panting for breath as she dragged the small man upright and held on to him. Her feet were freezing.

"You're a damned cop, I guess?" the man grumbled.

"No. I'm a private detective," she told him.

He made a sound and glared at her.

Logan and the hooker caught up, both laughing when they saw Kit with her prize in cuffs.

"Hey, a cop couldn't have done any better!" she said enthusiastically. "That looks like fun!"

"It is." Kit grinned. She held out her hand and the hooker shook it. "Thanks."

The hooker left and Logan propelled Kit to his car, one big hand wrapped completely around her arm while she held on to her bail jumper.

"Who's got who in custody here?" the little man asked.

"I've got you and he's got me, I guess." Kit sighed. "Just my luck. I can't even go on a stakeout on main street without ex-bosses popping out like measles."

"You mean you used to work for him?" the little man asked. "What a lucky escape you had!"

Logan scowled over his shoulder at the bail jumper. "Watch your mouth."

"Oh, aren't we in a nasty temper tonight," the prisoner mumbled.

"There's a policeman," Logan remarked, having spotted one.

"I can't . . . !" Kit protested, but it was already too late. Logan dragged her, and thereby the bail jumper, off to confront the officer.

"This man is a bail jumper," Logan said, propelling Kit and the man forward. "Can you tell me where to take him?"

"You aren't taking him anywhere . . . he belongs to me!" Kit raged.

"I do not," the bail jumper said indignantly. "You attacked me! Officer, this hooker attacked me and put me in handcuffs! I demand that you arrest her for assault!"

"I am not a hooker, I'm a private detective! Look, I have my ID right here . . . uh-oh."

She didn't. It was on her dresser at home, where she'd left it. She looked at the policeman, whose eyes were narrowing as he considered action. She looked at the bail jumper, who had a smug I'll-get-you-now look on his face. She glanced at Logan, who was obviously not concerned with trying to save her.

"Nice night," she remarked. "Well, toodle-ooh!"

She turned and took off, bare feet and all. There was a whistle and several shouts, but she kept running.

"Quick, in here!"

She followed the voice, and the hooker that she'd met earlier jerked her into the shadows of the alley.

"Now I'm in real trouble," Kit wailed. "I'm on the lam!"

"No. You're hiding from the heat."

"Oh. Sorry."

"Listen, go around the block and down the next alley, but go careful, you hear? I'll scout out the hunk and tell him where to find you."

"Thanks!" Kit said fervently.

"No problem. Run!"

She waved and darted through the alley.

Ten minutes later, Logan picked her up at the corner, the policeman having long since given up and taken the handcuffed man to headquarters to have his story checked. That wouldn't work to the agency's advantage, because Kit couldn't now claim that she'd collared him. But the client would have his money back just the same, and maybe Dane wouldn't fire her.

"Of all the harebrained, stupid stunts!" Logan shouted the minute he had her in the car. He turned the heater on full blast and pulled out into traffic. "You'll probably have pneumonia!"

"Go ahead, rub it in!" she muttered.

"I intend to, good and hard," he returned. "Do you have any idea how much trouble you could have found out there?"

"Of course I do, but it goes with the job," she replied. "Besides, I'm tough." She spoiled the pose with a loud sneeze, and wrapped her arms close around her shivering body.

"Tough, my elbow," he said heavily. "You're turning my hair gray."

"I'm not your problem," she reminded him, exasperated. "For heaven's sake, I don't even work for you!"

"My mother considers that you do. So does my brother."

"They don't count."

"They all blame me because you left."

"And you don't think they should!" she exclaimed.

He made an uncomfortable sound. "I must have been out of my mind to fire you," he said under his breath. "Nothing's been the same since. I can't find files, I can't get letters out the same day I dictate them, half my clients have quit because they think I'm running a brothel ..."

"A what?"

"The one who can spell tried to seduce the last three men who came into the office," he said icily. "I fired her!"

"Good for you. Who's doing the spelling now?"

"Cousin Melody. The smoker with acute bronchitis is now in the hospital. She says she won't come back."

"I don't blame her."

He glared in her direction. "You can keep quiet. One way or another, you've cost me plenty since you left."

"Since *you* fired me," she corrected.

He dragged a big hand through his thick hair. "Damn it, Kit, you know I never meant you to take it seriously! You never did before! My God, I fired you every other week, but you never actually left!"

"That was before Betsy came along and made vanilla pudding out of your brain," she replied stiffly.

"She didn't do anything except make me ache."

"While trying to pick your pockets," she said through her teeth.

"She isn't like that!" he raged, despite the fact that he was seeing Betsy with new eyes since he'd come back from San Antonio. In fact, he was discovering for himself that Kit was right and Betsy was exactly "like that." He wasn't admitting it, though. No, sir!

"The devil she isn't like that!" Kit shot back, turning in the seat. Her dark hair was damp and her mascara had run. Her hose had runs in them. She looked like a third-rate clown.

Logan couldn't help himself. He chuckled.

"That's right, laugh at me," she blustered. "You always found something about me to make fun of. If it wasn't my cat, it was a man I dated or something I wore...!"

"What ever became of the cat?"

She shrugged. "He moved to Detroit with a little girl down the street."

"Well, I'll be."

"He wasn't much of a cat, anyway. He ate half my potted plants before he left."

He shook his head, still laughing. "You have the most unorthodox life-style of anyone I know."

"You don't know me, Mr. Deverell," she told him flatly. "You never did. I was just a dictating machine with legs."

He glanced at her with a raised eyebrow. "Very nice legs, at that. You never bothered to display them at the office."

"God forbid that I should be accused of coming on to you," she taunted.

"That would have been the joke of the century." He turned the corner and eased the car into the underground garage at his apartment building. "I always did wonder why you were so nervous of being alone with me."

"You were forever yelling at me," she mumbled. "I wanted to have the door open so I could get a head start running if I had to. And why are we here? I'm not going up to your apartment with you!"

"You are," he replied grimly. "I'm not taking you home looking like *that!*"

"I left home looking like *this!*"

"I hope nobody saw you," he said curtly. "Or you may not have a home to go to."

"I went out the back," she said involuntarily. "I don't have anything else to wear...."

"I'll loan you a shirt and some jeans."

"Yours?" Her eyes imitated pie pans. "Great! Have you got some string so we can tie up the legs ... ?"

"Chris's would probably fit you. You're about the same build," he said with exaggerated patience. "I keep a change of clothing for him at the apartment in case he needs it."

"Why do you have an apartment and a house?" she asked, and then went scarlet at the look he gave her.

"Don't ask embarrassing questions if you don't want embarrassing answers."

"You can count on me, sir."

He helped her out of the car and into the elevator, careful to keep her out of sight beside his formidable bulk. Fortunately the hall was empty when they got to his floor. He whisked her into the apartment with an audible sigh of relief.

"Now just stay there while I—"

"Logan, are you finally home?" Betsy called half angrily from the bedroom. "I've been waiting for hours! Why didn't you call— Oh!"

Betsy was suddenly standing in the doorway of the bedroom, in a pink negligee. At the sight of Kit, her eyes bulged.

"You!"

"Hello, again, Betsy dear," Kit said prettily. "Logan brought me home for companionship, but since you're here..."

"Logan, how could you?" Betsy wailed, bursting into mock tears. "How could you?"

Logan cursed roundly under his breath. He threw off his overcoat. "Get into the shower while I fetch those clothes for you!" he told Kit. "In there, the guest room!"

He shoved her through the door and closed it with a loud thud. Afterward, there were loud voices and louder voices and thuds and silence and then a vicious slam. Kit got under the shower and used the fragrant soap to clean off her horrid perfume and makeup.

When she was scrubbed clean, she lifted a thick white robe from the back of the door and slipped into it. It must be Logan's, she thought. It smelled of the same sexy cologne he favored. She drew it closer while she wondered if she dared open the door. Betsy was probably still out there, waiting to cause an even worse scene.

Logan would want to get rid of Kit as soon as possible, she was sure, with Betsy waiting for him in all her glory. Kit could have screamed and wept, but it wouldn't help the situation. Betsy was in possession, and they all knew it. Logan might rescue Kit for old time's sake, but he wasn't emotionally involved. She wasn't stupid enough to mistake concern for love.

She opened the door and peeked around it. Logan was sitting sprawled in an easy chair, his jacket and tie off, his shirt open at the neck. He was sipping a glass of something amber colored. He looked broody and out of sorts. He was alone.

He spotted her and scowled. "Well, come on out of there," he said icily. "You've sure blown my evening to hell."

"You could go after her," Kit said miserably, her big blue eyes accusing. "I'm sure she'll get over it when you explain what happened."

"Explain?" he asked with a careless smile. The expression in his eyes wasn't careless; they were blazing. "Like hell I will! If she wants to take this at face value, let her. I don't give a damn."

"But, you must!" she protested. "You're engaged!"

He opened his palm and held out a huge diamond engagement ring. "Not anymore. Not since five minutes ago, thanks to you," he added with barely contained fury. He tossed the ring onto the coffee table.

She tugged the robe closer with a long sigh. "It's not my fault," she said miserably. "I never asked you to come storming into my stakeout."

He glared at her. "You think I could have left you there with a clear conscience?" he asked, exasperated.

"Yes, you could!" she muttered. She dug her hands deep into the pockets, aware of her bare feet and even barer body under the robe, her hair damp and tousled from the bath. "You don't have to wander the city at night looking for me. I'm not your responsibility."

He swirled the amber liquid in the glass, his big, dark eyes on her face. "So you keep telling me."

He looked older. There were deep lines in his broad face, and as she watched him sip whatever he was drinking, it occurred to her that she'd never seen him this way. Even when she'd traveled with him, there had always been a very formal atmosphere. He'd never taken off his jacket and tie in her presence, or done anything more than roll up his shirtsleeves. She'd learned more about him physically in San Antonio than she'd learned in three years.

In the intimacy of his apartment, she was more aware of him than ever. If only he loved her, wanted her, needed her, she thought miserably. If only there wasn't Betsy. As he'd said in San Antonio, she'd waited for years for him to notice her, and when he did, he'd turned the wrong way—toward Betsy, who was searching for a means of support, not a man.

"You look as worn as I feel right now, Kit," he said quietly, watching her as closely as she'd been watching him. "I don't suppose your evening was any bed of roses, either, even before I came along."

"I didn't realize what it would be like on the streets," she confessed, moving to sit on the sofa, poised on the very edge with her bare toes curling into the carpet. Her senses were all aroused, but still she felt at home with him, as if she belonged here. That was silly, and she pinched herself mentally. "Life is pretty terrible for some people, isn't it, Logan?"

"I suppose it is. You shouldn't have gone that far looking for your bail jumper."

"I know that, now," she admitted with a rueful smile. "I was gung ho on doing my job. Dane will probably fire me when he finds out what I did."

"Not Dane. He'll promote you for going above and beyond the line of duty." Logan laughed mirthlessly, his eyes slow and quiet on her face. "You've always given more than anyone asked of you. You used to stay late at the office night after night when I needed you, and I never heard you complain. I wasn't very kind to you, was I, Kit?"

"Why ruin your image on my account?" she mused dryly.

He chuckled. "I suppose it would have. I enjoyed our disagreements. I miss them."

"Hire someone who talks back."

"I tried. They run into the ladies' rest room when I start yelling." His big shoulders lifted and fell. "I suppose I'll have to learn to be polite."

"What a comedown."

"You don't know the half of it, honey."

He wasn't a man who used endearments, but that one sounded as if he meant it. In his deep, smooth voice it was seductive.

"I could go and talk to Betsy for you," she offered after a minute, because she did feel guilty.

His eyebrow jerked. "What would you tell her?" he asked curiously.

"The truth," she replied. "It seems to work best."

"After that blatant statement that you came back here to entertain me?"

"Well, I'm sorry about that," she said slowly. "It shocked me to find her standing practically naked in your bedroom."

"You might not believe it, but it shocked me, too. Since I came back from San Antonio, Betsy has been pushing me toward a quick ceremony, but I was resisting." He sipped his drink. "I think tonight was a dead-end play. She was going to make sure of me."

Kit flushed and looked away.

"Wouldn't you, if you were engaged to someone?" he persisted. "The risk of pregnancy would certainly be an incentive to an honorable man."

"You said you never took that kind of risk."

"Not normally. But any man can be pushed off balance by a seductive woman and driven crazy. Too crazy to give a damn about precautions."

She picked at the robe and didn't look up. "You don't seem the type to lose your head, Logan."

He smiled secretively and his dark eyes wandered all over her as though they were caressing hands. "Don't I, Kit? Well, why don't you take off that robe and I'll prove to you that I am."

Eight

Kit stared at him in disbelief. Perhaps she'd heard him wrong.

He didn't look as if he was kidding, though. His eyes were steady and very dark. Deliberately he put his glass on the table beside his elbow. He leaned back and slowly one big hand went to the buttons of his shirt and flicked them open. Under the shirt, his broad chest was darkly tanned and thick with curling black hair. He pulled the shirt out of his slacks and unfastened his belt. He tossed it aside, too, and then kicked off his shoes.

Still watching Kit, he stretched out full-length on the sofa with a cushion under his head.

"Come here," he said quietly.

There were, of course, fifty perfectly good reasons

to ignore him and lock herself in the bedroom. She went crazy trying to focus on any one of them. But with him lying there, sensuous and warm and welcoming, nothing in her brain seemed to work.

"Logan, I can't," she said hesitantly.

He didn't speak. He simply held out an arm.

She loved him. In the final analysis, there was nothing else that mattered, she told herself. Not the fact that he was on the rebound from Betsy, or that he didn't love her.

She got up and went to him. But when she sat down, he caught her arm and wouldn't let her any closer.

"The robe," he said, his voice deep and quiet and deadly somber. "Take it off, Kit."

"But, I can't . . . !"

"If you love me, you damned well can," he replied.

Her nerve gave out. He wanted more than she could give. What had she expected, anyway?

She started to get up, but his hands caught her wrists and held her there, gently but firmly.

"You only want consolation," she said. "I can't be an interlude or a diversion. I'm sorry. I . . . I want much more than that from a man before I can give myself," she added softly. "I'm not like Betsy."

His hands slid into hers, locking with them. He searched her eyes slowly. "I never had Betsy," he told her, his voice deep and still in the silent room.

She felt her cheeks going hot. "You were engaged to her."

"All the same, until tonight, she was intent on a legal ceremony beforehand."

"I see."

"I don't think you do. I know I didn't, until she perched there in her negligee and I realized for the first time that she was bargaining, not being moral." His eyes narrowed. "You wouldn't bargain with me, would you, Kit? You'd never use sex as a medium of exchange."

"I wouldn't know how," she said honestly.

"Little Miss Muffet," he murmured, studying her pixie face. He smiled. "All right, I won't seduce you. Is that what you want?"

She didn't. Her eyes fell to his chest and she wanted to feel her breasts burying themselves in that thicket of hair. Unfortunately he knew enough to realize that.

His big hand went to the knot at her waist and lingered there. He searched her eyes slowly, intently. "Despite all your hang-ups and principles, you want me. I could slide my hand inside this robe and touch your breasts, and you'd lie with me without a protest. I know that, and so do you. But I won't do it. If you sleep with me, you have to have both eyes open and no coercion about it."

"I suppose you know that I want to," she said miserably.

He nodded. "It's pretty hard to miss. What are you afraid of?"

"Everything," she said unhappily. "That you'll think I'm cheap, that I won't be able to live with it, that I'll get pregnant, that everyone will know..."

"I'll use something," he said curtly. "There will be no risk of your getting pregnant. No one will ever know except you and me. And for God's sake, how can I think you're cheap when you're a virgin?''

She lifted her eyes to his and smiled mirthlessly. ''Don't men always say these things to make women give in?''

''Of course,'' he admitted. ''Except that it's usually a casual arrangement with no strings attached. That isn't the case with you and me. You're in love with me. I know it. Do you think, under those circumstances, that I could ask you for a casual hour or two in bed to satisfy a passing urge? Do you think my conscience would let me?''

She hadn't expected the question and she couldn't quite answer it. She studied him without speaking while her mind whirled.

''Then . . . then what do you want?'' she asked.

''I want you to love me,'' he said huskily. ''I want to lie in your arms and be loved by you until I'm too exhausted to do anything except sleep.''

''Betsy . . . Betsy loves you.''

He shook his head. ''No. And you know it. I've never been loved. Not like you'd love me.''

''But it would only be one night . . .''

''Will you marry me, Kit?'' he asked.

Her body clenched. The thought was so ecstatic that her face burned with color. ''You don't want to marry me!'' She laughed nervously. ''Not for just one night!''

''It won't be for just one night. I'm thirty-five. You're twenty-five. We know each other much too well, in the important ways, not to get along.''

"An hour ago you were engaged to Betsy," she said through her teeth.

"Because you were so damned determined to save me from her that you pushed me right into her web!" he muttered. "My God, don't you know anything about men?"

"I know that they're selfish and manipulative and domineering!" she shot back.

"Who's domineering?"

"What do you mean, who's domi— Oh!"

He jerked her down against him and flipped her onto her back, taking her mouth with one slow, smooth motion. He groaned as he felt her lips part, felt the anger quickly transmuted into passion, and then into pleasure.

Her arms were under his, sliding around him, her hands caressing the hard, warm muscles of his back. She felt his heartbeat growing quick and erratic against the robe and then, without warning, against her bare breasts. The thick hair that covered him also covered her now, a soft abrasion that made her moan as he drew himself against her.

"Tell me to stop if you like, but do it now," he said over her mouth. "Hurry!"

His hands were on her, and she arched into them. "I can't," she whispered, shaken. "I don't want to! Logan... Please don't make me pregnant...!"

"I won't," he promised unsteadily. "I promise. Kiss me...!"

He drew her completely against him, so that she could feel the swollen contours of his body in passion. His hands threw off her robe and drew her hips into the curve of his body.

"Wait..." His mouth fastened hungrily onto her stomach and while he had her in thrall, he got his own clothing out of the way. When he slid back down against her, there was nothing between them, not even the air.

She wept, because the pleasure was so sweet and slow and terrible that she thought she wouldn't be able to bear it. His mouth on her body was heaven. His hands, touching her, exploring her, were ecstasy.

"The sofa... it isn't big enough for what we're going to do," he said against her mouth.

He moved and moved her, but he shuddered at the silken brush of her body and groaned. "I'll never make it to the bed," he whispered hoarsely.

She felt her back against the carpet and Logan's formidable weight above her. His mouth ground into hers as he slid over her, against her, his warm, hair-roughened thighs parting hers in a sensual movement that was as arousing as his tongue in her mouth.

"Here," he said roughly, pressing something into her hand. "Help me."

He taught her how, the touching intimate and exploratory as he whispered at her ear.

Then his kiss grew suddenly deep and demanding and his hips moved down. She felt him slowly invading her and she stiffened instinctively.

"Does it hurt?" he whispered.

"Not... not really," she whispered back, embarrassed by the question.

"Look at me." He forced her flushed face up and looked down into it as he moved with deliberate sureness. She gasped and clutched at him. The expression on her face aroused him beyond bearing. Submission was there, and need, and sudden understanding of what had been a mystery before.

"I'm going to take you," he said huskily. He moved, stilling her body with a firm hand. "I'm going to take you, Kit. Right now."

As he spoke, he arched down, and she gasped as she felt him completely possessing her.

She couldn't move, or breathe very well. He was heavy, but it was other sensations that she noticed. It was the heat of his skin, the beat of his heart, the pleasure that the rhythm began to build in her body. It was a trembling tension that slowly blocked out every single thought except the need to make it stop, any way she could.

She clutched his broad shoulders and her head thrashed. "Logan..." she whispered. "I can't...bear it, I can't...bear it!" she whimpered feverishly.

He laughed deep in his throat and moved harder. "Love me," he said, one big hand catching in the hair at her nape as he forced her to look at him. "Love me!"

"I...do!" Her eyes held his, bright with passion and love and spiraling pleasure. "Logan...I love you...more than my life!"

He blurred suddenly in her eyes as the harsh movements created a blinding red oblivion. She heard him speak, but her mind was totally intent on achieving satisfaction. She moved helplessly, her body demanding more than he was giving her, her voice pleading with him, sobbing as she climbed up and up and up.

The roughness of the carpet, the quick breathing, all blurred into a crescendo of movement and sudden throbbing stillness.

She sobbed helplessly as the waves swept over her, her voice mingling with Logan's harsh groans. Shuddering, they clung until the last trembling thread snapped and they spun away together.

He wouldn't let go. That registered as sanity came floating back. Kit opened her eyes and saw the ceiling over Logan's broad, damp shoulder. It wasn't quite steady. His heartbeat was rough against her breasts. His skin was wet and cold where it touched her.

"You made me whole," he said, shaken to his soul. His lips traveled softly over her face, her closed eyelids, her nose, her mouth, her cheeks, her chin. "Oh, God, Kit, you gave me ecstasy!"

"Yes." She smoothed back his damp, unruly hair, her eyes soft and serious as they met the black fever in his. "I love you," she whispered.

"I know. My God, how I know!" He kissed her with warm, slow passion, his body moving sensually above and within her. "It would be sacrilege to do that with another woman now!" he said under his breath.

"Would it, really?"

He lifted his head and smoothed back her soft hair tenderly. "You were with me every step of the way," he said huskily. "Every step! Do you have any idea how rare that is between lovers?"

She flushed and turned her shy face into his throat.

He laughed gently and held her there. "You're my lover," he whispered into her ear. "And I'm yours. After all these long years, we made love, Kit."

"You aren't sorry?" she asked worriedly.

"No. Are you?" he asked, lifting his head to study her.

She probably should have been, but she wasn't. She said so. Her fingers touched his hard mouth and she watched in wonder as he moved and she felt him, still a part of her.

"I know," he whispered at the expression on her face. "It awes me, too." He kissed her again, delighted in the feel of her body, the softness of her hair, the perfume that lay subtle and intoxicating on her throat. He groaned softly as the fever began to burn in him, but even as he felt the need, he denied it.

"No," he whispered on a shaken sigh. "No, we can't."

"Why?" she asked.

He told her, watching her blush. "And besides that," he murmured dryly, "I think you're probably going to be a bit uncomfortable for the next day or so. This takes getting used to."

"Oh."

He lifted away from her, poising there long enough to make her blush before he chuckled and rolled over onto his back. "Now you know," he murmured.

She sat up, wincing a little at the unfamiliar discomfort. He watched her and smiled with pure masculine triumph.

"I'll strut for a week," he murmured as she pulled the robe from the couch and wrapped up in it. "I could never have imagined the very prim and proper Miss Morris clawing my back raw and begging for satisfaction.''

"You can stop that," she said, hitting his chest. "Conceit doesn't become you."

"Yes, it does." He sat up and pulled her across his chest to kiss her roughly. "I've got you and I'm keeping you," he said, his dark eyes possessive and unblinking. "You'll never get away. First thing tomorrow, we're getting a license. As soon after that as possible, you're marrying me."

Her eyes mirrored her shock. "But...!"

"But nothing. Marriage is an honorable institution. I do have my reputation, and yours, to consider. Satisfying a passing urge is one thing, but what you and I just did, Miss Morris, has no relation whatsoever to fleeting lust. That, by God, was lovemaking. The real thing."

"I won't get pregnant." She faltered. "You took care of that."

"Kit, that isn't why I want to marry you."

"Oh. It's because you...deflowered me?"

"Deflowered?" he teased.

She glared at him. "What would you call it?"

"Delicious," he murmured against her mouth. "Sweet heaven. A taste of immortality. I could go on, but it would take weeks until I ran out of adjectives."

"Logan," she protested weakly.

"Are you hungry?" he asked softly. "I can cook bacon and eggs."

"I can cook, too," she replied.

He smiled at her, his eyes so warm and affectionate that she hardly recognized them. "We'll manage together. Then we'll sleep, in my bed, in each other's arms."

Her body tingled at the thought. Heaven seemed very close.

He got up and pulled on his slacks, holding out a hand to help her up. "Can you make cinnamon toast?" he asked, bending to kiss her gently.

"Yes."

He smiled. "Good. Come on. We'll share the work."

Breakfast at almost midnight wasn't at all bad, Kit thought. They washed up together, and that was nice, too. But the best part was lying with her head pillowed on Logan's broad chest in the dark bedroom, with the sounds of traffic outside. She curled into his body with absolute trust, so much in love, so happy, that she wanted to die if tomorrow meant giving it up.

He meant it about marriage. She didn't even question his motives. She loved him too much to say no. He wanted her, and there was something ... something ... in his expression when he looked at her. If it was only physical infatuation, it would wear off. She'd face that eventuality if she had to. But the look in his eyes gave her hope that it might be something more than an affair. She had that thought to cling to as she closed her eyes and went to sleep with the sound of Logan's breathing under her ear.

The next morning, she was aware of movement and sound as her eyes opened. She frowned, disoriented as she looked around. This wasn't her apartment, and it certainly wasn't her robe that she was sleeping in.

She sat up and looked around the room, and the night before came back to her in a flash of vivid impressions that made her face go rosy. She'd made love with Logan and slept in his arms all night. Now it was morning and time to pay the piper.

She got up and dressed in Chris's things that Logan had thoughtfully left on the chair, along with her flimsy, and by now quite dry, underthings.

"Are you ever going to get out of the bed and have breakfast?" came a disgruntled voice from beyond the door. "The eggs are congealing, for God's sake!"

"You're so impatient!" she muttered, throwing open the door.

He leaned against the jamb, tall and muscular and devastating in just slacks and a T-shirt with Atlanta Braves plastered across the front. "I wasn't last night," he reminded her wickedly.

She couldn't argue with that. She laughed up at him.

"You look very nice in Chris's jeans," he remarked, studying her trim figure. "Perhaps we could raid his closet while he's on vacation and see how you fill out the rest of his clothes."

"He probably looks much better in them than I do," she said.

"Not from where I'm standing. Come here." He lifted her by the waist onto a level with his big, dark eyes. "Kiss me, sweetheart," he whispered.

Tingling from the endearment, she leaned forward and put her soft mouth against his wide, hard one. "Good morning," she whispered back.

"Good morning yourself." He savored her lips, aglow with the wonder of having her this way, with the silky soft memory of the night before making him weak all over. He hadn't slept a long time. He'd woken long before first light and lay looking at Kit with wonder. So many years they'd been together, and he'd never seen how lovely she was. He really had been blind.

He kissed her slowly, barely brushing her mouth with his lips. "Come on and I'll feed you," he said. He put her back on her feet with flattering reluctance. "That isn't what I really wanted to do, of course. I want to throw you on the floor and ravish you, but it's much too early for that sort of thing. Besides, I'm too much a gentleman to seduce you on the floor of my apartment."

Remembering the carpet burns on her back she was hesitant to agree with him. He chuckled at her expression.

"Next time we'll use the bed," he murmured ruefully. "I couldn't hold out long enough to get into the bedroom."

"You said you weren't impatient?"

"I seem to have a low threshold with you, don't I?" He brushed back her short hair. "Are you sore, Kit?" he asked matter-of-factly.

"A little," she said nervously.

"There's nothing to be embarrassed about," he said gently. "I shouldn't have been quite so rough. I wanted you very badly."

"I wanted you, too."

"What a scarlet blush," he remarked. He smiled. "We'll eat and then we'll go apply for a license."

"It's Sunday."

"Is it? Well, we'll go apply for a license tomorrow, then." He seated her. "You can't make love again comfortably today, can you?"

She could hardly breathe. "I don't know..."

"There are ways, and ways," he whispered, bending to kiss her with soft tenderness. "I'll teach them to you."

He sat down beside her and poured the coffee. As they ate, Kit watched him and tried to imagine that he was the same man who'd been yelling at her for years over mistakes in dictation and fouled-up appointments and misfiled files—most of which were his own fault.

"Something bothering you?" he asked.

"It's really you, isn't it?" she replied vaguely. "I'm just having a little trouble believing it, that's all. We've worked together for a long time."

"And I've never looked at you until a few days ago," he agreed. His face went somber, almost grim. "I might have married Betsy. Why didn't you do something?"

"I did!" she shot back. "I tried to tell you, and you fired me!"

"I didn't know you were in love with me then," he said quietly.

"It wouldn't have stopped you if you had," she returned.

He didn't speak. His eyes were on his plate. "I haven't been very good to you over the years. I've been selfish and overbearing. Do you think you care enough to put up with me, Kit?" he asked, raising a curiously still face to hers. "Suppose you were only physically infatuated? After all, you knew nothing of men before last night."

Did he mean that? Or was he looking for a way out? She panicked and it showed in her eyes.

"Now what's wrong?" he asked gently.

"You're sorry about what happened, aren't you?" she blurted out.

"In a way," he had to admit. "I let you go to my head. I had no right to put you in that position. Despite the fact that I didn't let you get pregnant, you gave me something that you were saving for marriage."

"In which case, you would have had it anyway," she told him.

"Yes." He studied his fork. "But in the proper sequence. I find that I'm more conservative than I realized. I cheated you of a proper wedding night. I'm sorry."

"It wouldn't have been any different, really." She faltered. "I'd have been more nervous, I suppose..."

"You're still nervous." He caught her cold hand in his and warmed it. "Why?"

She couldn't quite explain it. "I'm shy, that's all. I've never slept with a man before."

He chuckled. "Are you sure it's that?"

She glared at him. "You don't have to make fun of me."

"Was I?" He sobered at once. "You're right. I shouldn't tease you about something that profound." His eyes slid down to the shirt she was wearing and lingered there until her breathing quickened. "I used to watch you sometimes and wonder what you looked like under your clothes. I was careful not to let you know, of course."

She smiled faintly. "I used to watch you and wonder what you looked like under your shirt."

"Now you know."

"Oh, yes."

Her eyes were faintly acquisitive. They made his body begin to throb all over again. He got up and stood over her. With a smooth motion, he pulled the T-shirt over his head and tossed it over a chair.

Kit's lips parted. "Oh, Logan," she whispered, her eyes as hungry as the hands she lifted to caress him with. "Logan, I love to touch you . . . !"

He groaned, lifting her into his arms. His mouth took hers roughly, claiming it. "I want you," he said harshly.

She clung, not protesting, as he carried her into the bedroom and came down beside her on the bed. She didn't say a word as he unfastened the shirt and removed it and her bra and leaned above her, studying her bare breasts with hot, hungry eyes.

"Make love to me," she whispered. "I want you, too."

"And hurt you?" he asked, forcing his eyes up to hers. "Because it would."

"I don't care," she told him. Her eyes smoothed over the broad, hair-roughened muscles of his chest. "I love you. It will be all right."

"You have a lot to learn about bodies and intimacy, little one," he said quietly. He held her eyes and unsnapped the jeans. The sound of the zipper was loud in the room. He slid his hand under them. "Let me show you what I mean."

He touched her, intimately, and watched her flinch. He wasn't rough. It was only that her body was new to passion, and very sensitized.

"You see, Kit?" he asked gently. "Remember how we were together last night, and try to imagine how it would feel when I went into you."

She went scarlet and gasped at the imagery.

"I know. It's blunt talk. But this kind of thing gets unmanageable. I can't start and then stop."

"No..."

He looked at her with aching need, his breath lodged in his chest as he withdrew his hand and smoothed it up her belly to her breasts and softly caressed them. "You are every dream I've had in my life," he whispered roughly.

With trembling hands she felt for a fastening and found it, moved it. His eyes widened and he gasped. His hand caught her wrist.

"No!" he said roughly.

"You want to," she breathed. She lifted her mouth

to his and kissed him, feeling his hold begin to slacken. "You know you want to, Logan. You want to...!"

He groaned and gave in to her. There were times, he thought blindly, when surrender was positively a virtue.

Nine

———

Logan drove Kit home late that afternoon, reluctant to let her go. But she'd insisted that she had chores to do, to get ready for work the next day.

"At lunch, we'll take out that marriage license," he told her firmly as he left her at her door. "You'll never get away again."

She smiled lovingly. "As if I'd ever want to," she said. "Am I dreaming?" she added somberly, searching his dark eyes. "I must be. I couldn't be this happy otherwise. I'll wake up..."

He was thinking the same thing as his eyes caressed her radiant face. "No, you won't," he said tenderly. He bent and brushed his mouth gently over hers. "I'll see you tomorrow."

"You aren't sorry?" she asked worriedly.

He stared at her for a long moment, seeing her with eyes that knew all about her. Everything. "Not if I died in my sleep."

"You're sure that you want to marry me?"

"Kit, do you think we've had enough of each other yet?" he mused. "I could go to you on my deathbed, don't you know? I'm in over my head, and so are you. Marriage is the only way for us."

"Your mother and brother..."

"Will be delighted. Especially my mother." He frowned. "Which reminds me. Kit, you have to find my mother."

"First thing tomorrow, I promise."

"My future wife, Jane Bond."

"How about Shirley Holmes?"

He chuckled. "Our kids will be born wearing trench coats and following the doctor around the delivery room."

She flushed. The thought of having a child was delightful—in wedlock. "I like children."

"I used to, before I got to know Emmett's," he said dryly. "I imagine we won't be so intimidated by our own." He frowned. "You were afraid last night that I might accidentally make you pregnant."

"Yes," she agreed. "I don't want to bring a child into the world without a stable relationship. I don't think you do, either."

"I don't suppose I do, Kit." He held her gently by the shoulders. "I'm no less conservative than you are, and I agree that children shouldn't be accidents. That's irresponsible."

She studied his face with eyes that adored it. "It's hard not to give in when you love someone," she said quietly. "I don't think I ever really understood losing control until last night. I couldn't say no. I couldn't stop."

"For what it's worth, neither could I. I'll take care of you, Kit."

"I'll take care of you, too," she promised.

He started to speak, but she put a soft hand over his mouth.

"It's not shameful to let a woman care about you and try to protect you," she told him.

He kissed her fingers. "Isn't it? All right." He sighed. "I'll work on it."

She smiled and reached up to kiss his square chin. "Good night, Logan."

"Good night."

The next morning, she started right out on her quest to find Tansy. But complications erupted before she'd even begun. Tess couldn't come in, so the office was shorthanded. And when she tried to find Tansy, the trail led to a medical center on the outskirts of Houston. To top off the confusion, Emmett and his three children came careening into the office just before Logan was due to pick up Kit.

"Emmett said we must come and see you, Kit." Amy grinned. Polk and Guy grouped around her as well, while a smug Emmett stood beside the desk with his white Stetson in hand, looking rather elegant in a gray business suit. The children were less presentable, though. Amy was wearing a stained and wrinkled dress. The boys had on jeans with holes at the knees and their hair needed washing.

"What are you doing here?" Kit asked, aghast.

"We came to see Tansy. She said we were welcome anytime," he added, his pale green eyes twinkling in his lean face, "and I'm in town for a rodeo. We thought the kids could stay with her while I work." He frowned. "But she's not at home."

"I'm looking for her," Kit said, without mentioning the medical center. She was reasonably certain that Logan didn't know about it, either, and until she found out what the problem was, she couldn't tell him. She didn't want him worried until there was something definite to worry about. Tansy might, after all, just be getting a checkup.

"She's done another flit, has she?" Emmett mused, pursing his firm lips.

"Looks like it. Oh, there's Logan!"

Logan came in the door, saw Emmett and the kids and began scowling.

"Hi, Cuz," Emmett said pleasantly. He rammed his hands into his pockets. "We came to stay with Tansy, but she isn't home."

"Don't expect to stay with me," Logan said with no hint of welcome. "I don't have room for you."

"Logan!" Kit exclaimed.

"Don't mind him," Emmett said imperturbably, smiling at Kit. "He's only jealous because he hasn't got any kids. Thought any more about marrying me, sweet thing?"

"She's marrying me," Logan said with a violent glare. He moved to Kit's side and caught her close. His sheer size was intimidating even without the black scowl he gave Emmett. "So get any thoughts in that direction right out of your mind."

"I was afraid it might come down to this." Emmett grimaced. "Ever since those kids overheard you two in the bathroom, I've expected to hear wedding bells."

Kit blushed and Logan glared at the grinning, innocent-looking children.

"Well, I've got to get signed up. What am I going to do with the kids?" Emmett groaned. "I was counting on being able to leave them with Tansy for the afternoon."

"Can't you take them with you?" Kit asked.

Emmett looked hunted, the kids snickered. "I did that last time I rode in a rodeo here. I'm afraid too many people remember them."

"I can't imagine why," Logan muttered darkly. "After all, having longhorn cattle standing in the middle of main street must be a common occurrence. Not to mention the two calves that invaded the local French boutique and tried on one of the designer dresses . . ."

Kit hid a smile. Emmett shrugged.

"Kids will be kids," he said, smiling fondly at his brood.

"Those aren't kids," Logan replied. "They're a commando group!"

"Thanks Cousin Logan!" Guy said with a grin.

"I have to leave them somewhere," Emmett repeated.

"Don't look at me," Logan said tautly. "I'm taking Kit to get a marriage license."

Emmett shrugged and looked so lost that Logan gave in. "All right. I know where we can leave them," he said, without mentioning that he was going to volunteer poor Melody. It was probably a terrible mistake, but there really wasn't anyone else available. Besides, Emmett had to face her sooner or later, and she had to face him. Today was a good time. "Come on."

"Logan . . . !" Kit protested squeakily.

"Keep quiet," he said under his breath, "or we'll get landed with them!"

Kit knew when to give up. She followed him out the door with the rest of them, waving discreetly to Doris as she left.

Melody was the only one left in Logan's office, with Harriet in the hospital and Margo gone permanently. She was bent over the computer, her long honey-streaked hair hanging down around her flushed face, wearing a trim beige suit that was stained with coffee and newsprint from the *Wall Street Journal.*

"May I help you . . . ?" she began, lifting soft brown eyes with a smile. She saw Emmett and the world tilted on its axis. Her expression was a study in quiet shock.

Emmett's normally pleasant, easygoing personality went into eclipse. He glared at her. He turned and stared furiously at Logan. "What the hell do you mean, bringing me here when she's in residence?" he demanded.

Melody swallowed, averting her eyes. "I work here," she said stiffly.

"You never said she was going to be permanent," Emmett told Logan, and there was frightening impact in those glittery green eyes when he turned to the other man. "What a hell of a relation you turned out to be, you damned turncoat!"

Logan glowered at him. "This is my office," Logan reminded him. "She's bright and capable, and I appreciate her talent."

"Her talent for what?" Emmett asked sarcastically.

"That isn't fair," Melody cried, glaring at him out of a white face. "It isn't fair at all! I had nothing to do with your divorce!"

"Your *brother* eloped with my wife!" he said through his teeth. "Do you think I can stand the sight of you?"

So that was it. No one had told her why Emmett clammed up when Melody's name was mentioned, but now she knew. Kit felt a surge of sympathy for Melody, who looked as if Emmett had struck her.

"It's hardly Melody's fault," Logan pointed out.

"Did our mother leave because of you, lady?" Amy asked.

"No!" Melody protested, coloring.

"But it was your brother who took her away!" Guy muttered.

"All of you, shut up," Kit said, intervening. She glared at Emmett, a little intimidated by that hard, unyielding countenance but determined to protect Melody. "No human being is responsible for the acts of another. It's terribly unfair of you to blame Melody for something her brother did."

Emmett didn't say another word. He glared at Melody. "I won't leave my babies with that woman."

"Who asked you to?" Melody asked through numb lips.

"Let's go, kids. You can come with me."

"I don't want to go to the arena," Polk muttered. "I hate cattle."

"You're the son of a rancher," Emmett began.

"I like computers, not cows." Polk went to the desk and stood beside Melody, refusing to budge. "I want to stay here."

"There's a television," Amy enthused, walking to the corner of the waiting room. She switched channels, "Look, *Sesame Street!*" She turned it up and sat down.

Guy glared at his brother and sister. "Turncoats. I'll go with you, Dad," he said, standing beside his father.

"That's my boy," Emmett said. He gave Melody a furious scowl. "Amy, Polk, let's go!"

Melody wanted to protest, but she could see that it wouldn't do any good. Emmett had despised her ever since he'd discovered her with his wife Adell and her brother Randy. She'd helped them pack and was standing with them while they caught a plane. There had been a terrible scene. Adell had cursed Emmett, and Emmett had cursed Randy and Adell and Melody roundly, for everyone to hear. It had been terribly embarrassing, especially for eighteen-year-old Melody.

She'd never forgotten her humiliation or her fear of Emmett, whose temper was legendary locally. He'd beaten Randy to a pulp before he'd stormed off, leaving Adell and Melody to patch up the cuts.

Melody hadn't seen him since, and that was deliberate. She'd moved to Houston to get clear out of his orbit. She'd taken the job with Logan because she knew Logan and Emmett never got along and didn't ever see each other. What a shocking development this was, to find Emmett here.

Amy and Polk rejoined their father. They looked dangerously vindictive.

"You'll be sorry, Emmett," Amy said sweetly. "I like Big Bird."

"You can learn to like cattle. Both of you. Let's go."

Emmett didn't put his foot down often. When he did, all three kids snapped to attention and did what was expected of them.

Emmett glared at Melody. "How long are you going to work here?" he demanded.

"For as long as she likes," Logan told him, getting between them. "It's no concern of yours. You live in San Antonio. Remember?"

"You hired her because of me," Emmett accused.

"I hired her because Tansy asked me to," Logan replied. "She's kin to us, you might remember, in a remote way. She was alone in Houston and needed work. I hired her." He looked at Melody and smiled reassuringly. "As it happens, I'm glad I did. She's an asset. Not up to Kit's record yet, but she's good."

"Words of praise from you?" Kit gasped. "I'll faint."

"Not yet," Logan chuckled. "I want your signature on a marriage license first."

Melody was frozen at her desk. The telephone rang and she answered it, capably if a little unsteadily.

"It's for you, Mr. Deverell," she told Logan. "Mr. James."

"Damn," Logan muttered. "I'll have to take it, Kit."

"That's all right."

He caught her hand. "Come on. I won't say anything you can't hear." He led her into the office and closed the door. A minute later, Melody heard him pick up and transferred the call.

Emmett was still glaring at her. She ignored him and went back to work, forcing her mind to the job at hand.

But her hands were trembling. Amy, who never liked other people, saw that and shyly approached Melody. "She's trembling," she said softly. She studied Melody's averted face and caught her breath. She glared at her father. "You made her cry, Emmett!"

"I'm not crying," Melody muttered, wiping her wet cheeks.

"But you are!" Amy protested. "Oh, you mustn't. Emmett didn't mean it. Did you, Emmett?"

"She helped your mother run away," Emmett said icily.

"That's right," Guy replied. "Come back here, Amy."

"But—"

Emmett's temper overflowed. "Damn it, I said let's go!" he shouted, his green eyes flashing at Amy.

Amy had never seen her parent so enraged. She obeyed him at once, a little afraid of the fierceness in his lean face.

Melody didn't look up as the door opened and then closed. She rested her hands on the computer keyboard and drew in deep breaths as she fought for control. She felt sick all over. The confrontation had been totally unexpected and shattering.

Logan and Kit came back out minutes later. By then, Melody was pale but composed.

"Mr. Deverell left," she told Logan.

"You know how bitter he is about Adell," Logan said gently. "Don't let him upset you. He'll be back on his way to San Antonio in a few days and you won't have to see him again. At any rate, it's unlikely that he'll come to the office anymore."

"Good," Melody said stiffly.

"He's a bitter man," Logan said. "I'm sorry he took it out on you. But it won't happen again."

"It's all right," Melody said. "Honestly."

"You're doing a good job," Logan told her. "I hope you'll stay."

"So do I," Kit agreed. "Even when we get married, I won't be coming back here to work. You're stuck."

Melody managed a laugh. "Then I'm glad. I enjoy the job. It's very interesting." She glanced at the door and gnawed her lower lip. "If you're sure that *he* won't be back."

"I'll guarantee it," Logan promised. "I'll be back about two. Can you cope?"

"Yes, sir," Melody promised him.

He smiled, and escorted Kit out the door.

"Emmett is a . . ." she began hotly.

"Yes," he said, leading her to the elevator. "I've never seen him be so savage with anyone like that," he added. "Least of all someone as young as Melody. My God, what a temper!"

"He takes after the rest of the Deverells," she said dryly.

He glared at her. "I don't pick on young women."

Her eyebrows raised over stark open eyes. "What do you think I was when I came to work for you, you slave-driving tyrant?"

"I am not a tyrant," he said, pushing the Down button hard. "I was terrific to work for."

"When?"

He narrowed his eyes as he studied her. "Do you want to marry me or not?"

"Of course I do."

"Then be nice to me."

She moved close, glancing down the deserted hall. "How nice do I have to be?" she whispered, and suddenly plastered herself against his big body.

He chuckled and pushed her away. "Not that nice," he told her. "Not until it's legal, anyway. From now on, we're doing it by the book."

"Party pooper."

"All right, if you really want to make love on the floor of the elevator . . . !"

"No!"

He laughed delightedly as she backed away from him. "Well, what did you expect? I'm pretty vulnerable with you."

"So I noticed." She fanned herself with her hand. "And you a respectable stockbroker, too."

"I'm an engaged man. Damn this sluggish elevator...!"

The door opened finally, and a broody, muttering Emmett and three red-faced children stared out of it at Kit and Logan.

"Now what?" Logan asked curtly.

"Big Bird," Emmett said through his teeth.

"What?"

"She incited them." He gestured toward the other two. "They're in it all together. They stood in the middle of the sidewalk and told God and the rest of the world that I was stunting their natural development by denying them educational programming. Then," he added viciously, "they overturned a fajita stand and dumped salsa on a fat lady."

Kit leaned against the wall, laughing so hard that she could barely stand.

"Well, you needn't look at me," Logan told his furious cousin. "I'm not keeping them for you. And if I were you, I wouldn't go near Melody. She'll probably throw a keyboard at you if you so much as stick your head in the door!"

"I'm not stupid," Emmett replied. "Go on," he told the kids. "I hope she stuffs you into a drawer!"

"I don't want to go!" Guy muttered. "She stole our mother!"

"This isn't the time or the place," Logan said. "Go on, Guy. Try not to upset Melody anymore, if you please. Your father's done a great job on her nerves already."

"All right," Guy muttered. He glanced back at his father. "But I'm on your side, Dad."

"I know that," Emmett replied quietly. "Go on. Don't...give her any trouble." He shrugged. "I guess I was pretty obnoxious."

"That's an understatement," Logan said as he got into the elevator with Kit and a subdued Emmett. "She's terrified of you, couldn't you tell? Two years have passed since you beat her brother to his knees and verbally assaulted her, and she still starts shaking the minute she sees you. Quite a feat, cousin," he added venomously, watching Emmett shift his eyes. "You didn't use to stoop to terrorizing children."

"She isn't a child," Emmett said stiffly.

"But she is. She's barely twenty," Kit said quietly. "And she isn't worldly at all."

Emmett scowled. "Twenty?"

"You didn't know?" Kit asked, staring up at him curiously.

His broad shoulders rose and fell. "I never thought about it." He went broody, avoiding Logan's sudden stare.

They left him on the sidewalk and went to get into Logan's sleek Lincoln.

"Is Emmett really like that?" Kit asked. "He seemed so easygoing and kind..."

"He's a hell-raiser," Logan told her as he put her into the car and got in beside her. "He always was wild, even as a boy. He married Adell just days after his mother died and he insisted that they start a family right away. She seemed to care about him, and we thought he'd settled down. But he took off rodeoing and left her there alone with babies and cattle, and she was never suited to either. She met Randy, fell in love for real and just took off. Emmett blamed her, blamed Melody, blamed the kids, blamed everybody except the real guilty party—himself. He hated marriage and responsibility. He was trying to find a way out when Adell presented him with one. His pride was bruised, but he never loved her.''

"He got married because of what happened to his mother?''

"Yes, I think he did. He was lonely and Adell thought she loved him. It was only infatuation, though.'' He stopped at a traffic light and looked at Kit worriedly. "Do you love me?'' he asked suddenly. "Do you love me enough, Kit?''

Her lips parted as she studied his broad, leonine face. "I'd do anything in this world for you,'' she said quietly. "Anything, Logan.''

That didn't sound like infatuation, and combined with the look in her eyes he was convinced. He took her hand in his as the light changed and wrapped it in his fingers. "That's all I wanted to know.''

Which told Kit very little about his own feelings. It was impossible not to know how much he wanted her. As he'd said, they did get along well together. But what if he discovered one day that what he felt for Kit was only a physical infatuation? What if he fell in love with someone else and took off?

"Stop brooding,'' he said, smiling at her. "We've got plenty going for us. We'll make it, Kit. I promise you, we will.''

Her long fingers curled into his. "Okay. I won't worry."

But she did worry. They took out the license and she went back to the office to continue her search for Tansy. It was much more imperative now to find her, with the impending marriage. She wanted Tansy there. More, she wanted to make sure that her future mother-in-law was all right. The fact that Tansy had checked into a medical center was very worrying indeed. Usually when the elderly woman sought medical assistance, it was after some wild stunt that bruised her. But there hadn't been any wild stunts. Tansy had gone in deliberately, on both feet. And that in itself, Kit thought uneasily, was cause for concern.

Ten

Kit found the hospital without a problem. Then she sat in the car, worrying about how to proceed. There was a good chance that Tansy would be very angry if Kit just walked into her room and started asking questions. On the other hand, there was little else she could do.

Leaving her car in the parking lot, she proceeded into the hospital and found which room Tansy was in. She hesitated outside the private room, but only for a minute. With a deep breath, she knocked gently at the door and opened it.

Tansy Deverell stared at her without speaking, her eyes very wide in a thin, pale face which held pain and worry.

"And here you come again," Tansy murmured, with a hint of a twinkle in her eyes.

"Yep," Kit said, smiling.

"You're too good a detective, Kit," Tansy said. "This time I didn't want to be found."

"I had that figured out for myself." She moved to the bed, and sat down beside it, her blue eyes quiet and steady on the worn face in its frame of untidy silver hair. "Why are you here?"

"I won't tell you that."

"Are you ill?"

"I won't know that until I get the results of the tests."

Kit held her breath. "Tests for what?"

Tansy couldn't conceal her worry and fear. "I don't know, Kit," she said in a choked tone. "I've been getting tired a lot, and I can't seem to stop losing weight. I don't know, but it could be cancer."

"Oh, Tansy," Kit wailed.

"And if it is," she continued, "I don't want my boys to have to suffer through the uncertainty with me. When I find out for sure, then I'll tell them."

Kit felt terrible. She knew she should tell Logan and Chris, but Tansy looked crushed enough already.

"It isn't fair to keep it from them," Kit began gently.

"Yes, it is, dear," came the soft reply. "You're all heart, aren't you, Kit?" she asked. "Nothing like that curvy cash register he thinks he's in love with."

"The delectable Betsy?" Kit replied with a quiet smile.

"Chris's description." Tansy nodded and she smiled. "He'll come to his senses one day."

"I'm delighted to tell you that he already has," Kit told her. "We just got a marriage license. I'm going to be your daughter-in-law."

Tansy held out her arms and hugged the younger woman with pure delight. "You couldn't have brought me happier news if you'd looked for years. Kit, how wonderful!"

"He doesn't love me yet," Kit told her. "But maybe I love him enough for both of us."

"Give him time. Commitment is new to him. He's my son. He can't be completely stupid."

Kit laughed. "Of course he can't."

Tansy could sympathize with Kit. It was hard to love so deeply and not have it returned. If only her eldest son wasn't so blind!

She rubbed her cold hands. "Go away, Kit. I love seeing you, but this is something I have to do alone. And don't tell my sons. Not a word," she said sternly.

"But..."

"Not one word," Tansy repeated, her eyes piercing. "This is my business. Mine alone."

Kit knew when she was beaten. "All right. But I'll be back to see about you," she said firmly.

"I knew that already," Tansy said, and smiled. "You're a sweet child."

"No. I just have good taste in people," Kit murmured.

Tansy laughed, although her eyes didn't.

"When will you know, one way or the other?" Kit asked.

"Tomorrow."

"Then I'll see you tomorrow. Can I bring you anything?"

"Not really, Kit. But thank you for asking."

She studied the older woman, noticing that her hands were shaking. "Tansy..."

"I'm freezing," Tansy said. "And starving to death. You know, no matter how much I eat or drink, I can't seem to get full. All that hunger and thirst, and look at me." She laughed. "Skin and bones." She lay back and closed her eyes. "Life is so complicated sometimes."

"Don't we all know it," Kit mused.

"How is Melody working out?"

"I don't know if he'll still have her by sundown," Kit replied. "She's baby-sitting Emmett's kids, and he hates her. I mean hates her!"

Tansy's eyes opened and she looked less frail. "Oh, my goodness. Poor child!"

"She's a trooper. Amy and Polk like her. Guy is his father all over again. I imagine he's giving her the devil."

"She's too young to bear the brunt of Emmett's hatred of her brother. I shouldn't have recommended her for the job, but she'd just lost a job she'd had for two years and she was too afraid of Emmett to even live in the same city he did. I saw a chance to help Logan and Melody. But if Emmett is going to make a habit of coming back here, I may have done more harm than good. Poor child!" she repeated.

"Emmett didn't even look like himself," Kit said, recalling with a mental shiver. "I thought he was easygoing and funny."

"Did you? Emmett wears a mask. Most people see through it a lot sooner than you did. He has plenty of enemies."

"If he's like he was today when he rides in a rodeo, it wouldn't surprise me to learn that he wins every event," she said. "He's ruthless."

"He always was. It's his way or no way." Tansy shook her head. "I'll have to apologize to Melody. But Emmett won't be in town for long, I'm sure. Logan will protect her."

Kit wasn't certain about that, but she didn't say so. She stayed and talked for a little longer, before she looked at her watch and realized that she was already past due back at the office.

"I have to go," she said, bending to kiss the thin cheek. "You know where to find me if I can do anything for you. And I won't tell Logan or Chris where you are. I promise."

Tansy studied her face for a long moment, reading accurately the acquiescence in it. "That's a deal. Come back tomorrow. Maybe it will be good news."

She didn't sound as if she expected it to be. Kit was an incurable optimist, though, and she knew what a strength of will Tansy had.

"I'd bet on you, no matter what," she told Tansy. "You're too special to lose." She smiled and left the room before Tansy had time to reply.

It didn't help that later in the day Dane Lassiter wanted to know about her progress.

She considered lying to him. That didn't seem particularly bright. Dane was a detective himself, and much more experienced. If he wanted to find Tansy, it would take him no time at all. And it would be dishonest to lie.

So she asked to speak to him privately and told him everything.

"So you see," she said miserably, "I don't know what to do. I told Tansy I wouldn't tell Logan a thing. Professionally I'm bound to." Her eyes searched his stern face. "Where do you draw the line?"

"In this agency, we stand behind our detectives," he said, smiling gently. "It's your decision."

"Thanks for not firing me." She got up from the chair she'd been sitting in.

"Don't be absurd," he murmured. "I trust your judgment." He sighed. "God, I hope it's not cancer. Logan pretends that his mother is a trial to him, but he loves her."

"So does Chris," she added.

"Of course he does. But Logan will take it harder."

She nodded. He was right about that. The icy Mr. Deverell had a surprisingly soft side, and he did adore his mother. Even if he raised the roof over some of her antics from time to time.

"Kit," Dane said as she started to leave, and he looked solemn, "think very carefully about the position you're putting yourself in. You and Logan are engaged. Keeping this sort of secret between you could irreparably damage your relationship. I won't blame you if you do give in and tell him. No one would, least of all Tansy."

"I don't know about that." She clung to the door. "If I tell Logan, I'll be betraying Tansy's trust."

"It's a hard decision, I know," Dane said. "Just remember, you have to live with the consequences of your actions. I don't. Neither does Tansy."

"Yes. I know," she said quietly.

Kit had hoped that she wouldn't have to lie to Logan. The following day, after all, she'd know for certain about Tansy. But she had no such luck.

Logan telephoned less than ten minutes before she was due to leave the office that afternoon. In the background, boisterous yells and shouts interrupted him.

"I'll pick you up about six and we'll eat out," he said. "Can you kids shut up?" he yelled. "My God, they're driving us nuts! Emmett promised to be back by five, and he isn't here! I don't know what to do!"

"Bring them with you," Kit suggested, buying time. "We can look after them."

"Kit, are you out of your mind?" he asked.

"I guess so. But we can't ask Melody to have them, not the way Emmett treated her."

"I know." He paused. "Have you found my mother?" he asked abruptly.

The question shook her. She took a slow breath and steadied her nerves, preparing to hedge the question. She was flirting with finishing their relationship before it began, and she knew it, but Tansy trusted her. She had to consider that before she considered her personal feelings.

"I've got a good lead that I'm following up," she replied carefully, mentally crossing her fingers at the lie. "I should know something by lunch tomorrow," she added, praying that she would, and that it would be good news.

"I thought you were an ace detective, Miss Morris."

"Detective work can be slow, Mr. Deverell," she countered. "And you might remember that I am very efficient."

"So you were." He chuckled. "Come on over here and go home with me. We can pick up your car in the morning."

"Okay. I'll be there in fifteen minutes," she promised.

She and Emmett arrived together. He was unusually quiet as he rode up in the elevator with her, totally uncommunicative.

"Did you get signed up for the rodeo?" she asked.

"Yep."

And that was all he said, all the way to Logan's office. He walked in, saw the kids sitting all in a row on the sofa with their hands angelically folded and did a double take.

A harassed, black-eyed Melody glared at him. "You can take them with you, now, if you don't mind," she said stiffly. "I hired on here to be a secretary, not a baby-sitter."

"We ain't babies," Guy muttered with a hard glare in her direction. "And we ain't scared of that electronic gadget in your desk, neither!"

"What electronic gadget?" Emmett said with deadly menace.

Melody looked straight at him, opened her desk, picked up a black box and pointed it at him. She pressed a colorful button. Death ray sounds out of a Grade-B science fiction movie filled the room.

"Tomorrow morning when you wake up, you'll have green skin and antennae," she promised him. "And warts."

Emmett's eyebrows lifted.

"She tried to turn us into Martians with that thing, but we weren't scared of it, Emmett," Amy said proudly. Her haughty expression wavered just a little when she glanced at the black box. "But, we'll go now, won't we? Before she points it at us again, I mean."

"Witch," Emmett accused. "Scaring little children."

Melody put the black box back in the drawer. "Those aren't little children," she said icily. "They're a homebound terrorist unit, complete with hardware. Look at this, for heaven's sake!"

She started pulling things out of the desk. When she finished, there were screwdrivers, Swiss Army knives, fingernail files and other assorted tools in a heap before her. "Just look! They could break open a safe with this!"

"No, we could not," Polk said indignantly.

"We only tried one," Guy reminded his brother. "And it was old. If we worked on a new one..."

"That's right!" Amy agreed.

Exasperated, Melody stared at Emmett. "Congratulations," she said. "You can visit them all in federal prison next year after you're through riding in rodeo competitions.''

Emmett stared at his children. Comprehension was dawning. He'd spent two years hating his ex-wife and blaming her for all his problems. He'd spent an equally long time running away from the kids.

Now, here they were, and he was just beginning to see what his neglect had accomplished. Instead of normal, wholesome children, he was raising a family of potential second-story men.

''Where did you kids get that stuff?'' Emmett asked, nodding toward the desk.

''We'll never tell,'' Amy said, making a motion across her lips like a zipper closing.

''That's right,'' Polk agreed.

''We'll see about that,'' Emmett said grimly. ''Let's go. I've booked us into a hotel for the night.''

''Great!'' Guy said. ''At least we can escape the wicked witch of the stock market before she makes Martians out of us.''

Emmett herded them to the door. He paused, glancing at Melody, who was composed and not very communicative. ''Kind of you to watch them,'' he said reluctantly.

''I'll quit before I do it again, even if it means starving,'' she said quietly.

His lean face hardened. ''No stomach for children, Miss Cartman?''

''I like most children,'' she replied.

''There's not a damned thing wrong with those kids,'' he said furiously.

She didn't reply.

"Emmett, that's enough," Logan said with quiet menace. "Go away."

"You hired her to get back at me, didn't you?" Emmett accused his cousin.

"You think everyone is out to get you, don't you?" Logan asked quietly. "Your biggest problem is your own lack of trust."

"I trusted Adell. Until *her* damned Romeo brother," he pointed at Melody, "waltzed in and carted her off!"

Melody colored. Her hands were shaking. She clasped them together tightly. "Adell said she got tired of dirty diapers and living alone with three toddlers," she said with pure bravado and a shaking voice, "while you strutted around with pretty young girls at rodeos."

Emmett didn't say another word. His face hardened to stone. He turned and went out, slamming the door so hard that the windows shook.

"Well, he did," Melody muttered, shaken.

"I know," Logan replied. "You don't have to tell me about Emmett. I'm sorry, Melody. I won't let him in here again."

"Thanks," she said quietly. "I seem to set him off."

"Everything does. Get your things and I'll lock up. I'm taking Kit out to eat. Want to come along?"

Melody smiled. "Thanks, but I've got a nice pot full of soup waiting."

"That sounds good on a cold night," Kit remarked.

"Well, good night, Melody," Logan said.

* * *

Logan took Kit to an elegant restaurant and they drank expensive wine and ate perfectly cooked steak, paying much more attention to each other than to the food.

"Two more days," he groaned when he kissed her good-night at her door. "I'll never make it!"

"Yes, you will," she said, smiling with delight at his hunger for her. "Good night, Logan."

He kissed her one last time and reluctantly let her go. "Good night. If you find out anything about Tansy, call me, all right?" he added.

She cleared her throat and averted her eyes. "Certainly I will!"

Logan saw that suspicious, guilty look and scowled. "You aren't holding anything back, are you?"

"Logan!" she exclaimed. "Of course not."

He stuck his hands into his pockets and stared down at her, frowning. "I love my mother, despite her shenanigans," he reminded her. "If you know something, and you don't tell me, I won't forget it."

Her conscience was killing her. She wanted to tell him. She should tell him. But she couldn't force the words out. She groaned. "There's nothing to tell yet," she said.

"When?"

"Soon. Really."

He nodded, but his eyes were watchful. And there was a blatant withdrawal in his manner when he turned and walked away from her.

She closed the door behind him, locked it and leaned back against it. Her heart was beating her to death with its mad rhythm. Blast her own tongue! She wasn't good at lying. Now Logan was suspicious, and Tansy would never forgive her if he found out anything too soon. But, then, how could he?

By the time she went to bed, she'd convinced herself that he had no way of knowing that she wasn't telling the truth. And Dane wouldn't blow her cover. No, she had nothing to worry about.

Late in the morning, after she'd gone through her files and done some legwork on an unrelated case, she drove to the hospital and went to find Tansy.

She knew by the expression on the older woman's face that it wasn't cancer.

"You're all right, aren't you?" she asked Tansy, smiling. "It wasn't cancer after all, was it?"

"No," Tansy sighed, smiling. "Thank God, it wasn't."

The door opened suddenly and Logan Deverell came in, his face like a thundercloud. "So here you are," he told Tansy. "Hiding out in a hospital...what's wrong with you?"

Tansy stared at Kit and grimaced. "You told him! You told him, after I begged you not to!"

"No," Kit began.

"Why are you here?" Logan demanded from his mother.

Tansy glared up at him. "I thought I had cancer."

He went stark white. "And...?"

"It's not," she said shortly.

His dark eyes, relieved, went to Kit's white face and kindled again. "You lied to me, damn you," he said softly. "You told me you didn't know where she was!

She's been in here with the threat of cancer hanging over her and I wouldn't have known!''

Kit didn't reply. She couldn't. She felt as bad as he must.

"Oh, Kit, I'm sorry," Tansy began.

"Dane's going to get an earful about this, and I damned well hope he fires you!'' he said, bristling with rage at her betrayal. He'd trusted her, planned to marry her. But she didn't trust him. She'd covered up his mother's situation and her hospitalization. She'd deliberately lied to him about it! He was so furious that he could barely speak.

"Get out of my mother's room!'' he said viciously. "Get out of my life, while you're about it! You can take that damned marriage license and rip it up, because I wouldn't go five feet toward the altar with a two-faced, cold-blooded little liar like you!''

Kit felt the tears welling in her very soul. They both blurred in her blue eyes as she turned and went out of the room with the tatters of her dignity around her.

"But it's not her fault," Tansy was saying loudly.

She didn't hear what Logan said. She kept walking.

Eventually she found her car, through a mist of hot tears. Her eyes were red and swollen long before she got back to the office and went to tell Dane Lassiter what had happened.

Tess was with him. They both gaped at the sight of her.

She blurted out the whole story and then dried her eyes and blew her nose. "He wants you to fire me,'' she told Dane. "I guess I deserve it. I was only trying to do what Tansy wanted me to, but she wasn't paying us, Logan was. He said he had the right to know."

Tess hugged her warmly. "Now, now," she said soothingly. "It's all right."

"I'm not going to fire you," Dane said. "If Logan wants to refuse to pay, that's his affair. The agency won't lose that much. But he will," he added curtly. "The next time Tansy takes a powder, he can damned well track her down himself."

"Not on my account," Kit pleaded. "I don't want any of you in trouble because of me."

"You're our employee," Dane said curtly. "That makes you family. Nobody, but nobody, threatens family around here."

Kit forced a smile. "You're very kind."

"It's easy to be kind to nice people. You go back to work and get your mind on another case. Consider this one closed."

"Okay. Thanks," she added.

"We're going shopping tonight," Tess reminded her. "It will cheer you up."

"I could really use that now," Kit replied.

She went back to her desk. Adams paused beside it, frowning. "You okay?" he asked. "I heard Deverell took a bite out of you. Don't let it get you down. We all catch hell sometimes, you know." He grinned sheepishly. "Want me to go bash his nose in for you?"

She laughed, her blue eyes twinkling. "Would you do that for me?"

He blushed. "Sure. If you want me to."

She reached out and took his big, hammy hand in hers. "Adams, you're the nicest man in the world."

He only smiled, looking even more sheepish.

"How about supper?" he began. "Doris and I know this place that makes great Irish stew," he added, glancing at Doris, who smiled and nodded. "You could have supper with us..."

The sound of the front door opening caught their attention. The person entering had full view of Adams holding Kit's hand and smiling at her.

Logan Deverell stared at them from a face that would have done justice at a murder trial.

Kit's eyes sparkled with anger. Her injured dignity sat up and growled. "Yes, Mr. Deverell, can we help you?" she asked. "If you'd like to speak to Mr. Lassiter, I'm sure he'll be happy to oblige you. I've already told him that you're dissatisfied with my handling of your case. Sadly for you, he doesn't feel it warrants firing me."

"This the guy you were telling me about?" Adams asked Kit, looking big and pugnacious, an expression he'd cultivated back in his homicide days on the police force.

Logan glared at Adams. "I hope your medical insurance is paid up," he said levelly, "because I'm a Tae Kwon Do blue belt."

"I don't need a bodyguard, thanks just the same, Adams," she added, gently disengaging her hand.

"Well, if you do," Adams said, glancing toward Logan, "just whistle."

He ambled away and Logan shoved his hands into his pockets as he moved to stand just in front of Kit's desk. His broad shoulders rose and fell. "Mother told me all of it." He looked uncomfortable. "I shouldn't have jumped to conclusions."

"If that's an apology, it isn't necessary," Kit began.

"Isn't it?" His dark eyes slid over her face. "You've been crying."

"Tansy was angry with me," she hedged.

He scowled. "Was that the only reason?"

She lowered her gaze to her locked fingers, lying cold on her desk top. "How is she?"

"Diabetic, apparently," he said. "They've had to put her on insulin. That explains her weight loss and the gnawing hunger and thirst and weakness. They're sure she'll be back in top form in no time."

"Did it come on suddenly?"

"Apparently not. But she didn't recognize the symptoms. She was thin for years, and then she started to gain weight. They said she was a textbook Type II diabetic who could be controlled with diet. Her penchant for sweets put her over the line." He shifted. "It may have saved her life. She very nearly went into a coma."

"Poor Tansy."

"In more ways than one. She felt guilty about you. I caught hell for what I said to you," he mused, smiling faintly.

She refused to rise to the bait. She was tired of being cut to pieces by him. She lifted a composed face. "Did you want to see Mr. Lassiter? Our receptionist is still out of the office, but I can buzz him for you."

"No, I don't need to see Dane," he replied. "He can bill me for services rendered, no argument. You found her. It's her fault I wasn't told, not yours.'' He searched her weary face. ''You're very loyal, Kit.''

She didn't react. ''If that's all,'' she said without expression, ''I have another case I need to be working on.''

''A case, or Adams?'' he asked with a speaking glance in the general direction of the office where Adams had disappeared.

''Adams is . . .''

''As Nick used to say, a tick,'' he said, lowering his voice. ''If he attaches himself to you, you'll never get rid of him.''

''That's my business, Mr. Deverell,'' she reminded him. ''You have no right to interfere in my personal life.''

He recognized the quote, and she'd meant him to. He pursed his lips. ''Throwing my own words back at me?'' he asked. ''I suppose I don't deserve any less.''

She didn't reply.

He searched her blue eyes for a long moment, and delicious sensations shot through his powerful body as he let the look linger. Kit blushed and averted her face, and his heart jumped in his chest.

Three years, he thought. He'd never really looked at her. He'd never let himself look at her. Now she was out of his office, out of his life, and he couldn't seem to stop looking at her. Betsy had been a remedy for boredom, but Kit was . . . everything. He looked down at her and loved her, suddenly, unbearably. He'd given her hell for something that wasn't her fault, broken their engagement. And after all that, to discover that he was in love with her . . .

He shrugged. His eyes slid over her body. "Tansy wants to see you."

She nodded. "I know where she is."

"I really am sorry," he said unexpectedly. "I was thinking that you'd betrayed me, that you hadn't trusted me enough to be honest with me. I . . . lost my temper."

"I noticed."

"Damn it, Kit, you have to marry me!" he burst out.

"Why?" she asked haughtily, aware that everyone in the office was staring at them.

He looked around at the audience and sighed furiously. "Don't you all have anything better to do?" he demanded.

"Not me," Adams said. "How about you guys?"

The other detectives and skip tracers shook their heads.

"Oh, hell," Logan muttered. He rammed his hands into his pockets and looked down at Kit with pure repressed fury.

"What does it matter to you that you broke the engagement?" Kit asked. "You never wanted to marry me in the first place. I was just a substitute for Betsy!"

Logan searched her flushed face and couldn't drag his eyes away. She was so lovely. He remembered her laughing, and crying, and he knew that nothing would fill the gap in his life if she left him.

"Actually, Kit, it was the other way around," he said finally. "Betsy was a substitute—and a very poor one, at that—for you."

Eleven

———

"That isn't true," Kit said quietly.

"Isn't it?" He moved to the desk and stood over her. "Did you tear up the marriage license?"

"I meant to," she returned.

"Where is it?"

She hesitated. She reached into her desk drawer and pulled it out. They'd had the blood test the same day they'd taken out the license. They could be married legally today.

"Come on," he said gently. "Let's get married."

"But, Logan," she protested.

He drew her out of her chair. "City hall, eleven o'clock," he told the office. "You're all invited!"

There were so many congratulations and well-wishes that Kit couldn't get anyone to listen when she said it was a mistake, and she wasn't marrying Logan.

It did no good to try. He put her into her coat, took her out the door and drove her down to city hall.

"But what about Tansy?" she groaned.

"We'll go and see her afterward," he replied. "She was delighted when I phoned her."

"You didn't know that I'd have anything to do with you after this morning," she said icily.

"I knew that you loved me," he said simply. "If I've learned nothing else in life, it's that love doesn't wear out."

"Mine might have. You starved it."

"Yes. And now I'm going to feed it until it becomes overweight," he promised. "Ten minutes after you say I do I'm going to take you to our apartment and make love to you until you're too weak to walk!"

She flushed. "Hush!" she exclaimed, glancing around.

"We can make love on the carpet, like we did the first time," he said imperturbably. "Except that this time, it's going to be very, very different."

"Because you've resigned yourself to marriage?" she asked dully.

He turned her face to his and held her eyes. "Because I finally woke up and realized what was happening to me. I love you, Kit," he said with quiet wonder, searching her shocked face. "I suppose I did all along. But I didn't know it until I broke the engagement and sent you running out of Tansy's hospital room. I worried that you might have taken me at face value, that I wouldn't be able to get you back."

"You love me?" she asked, staring at him blankly.

"Oh, yes," he said huskily, putting more feeling into the words than she'd dreamed anyone could. "Can't you see it? Feel it?"

She could. Her heart ran wild. "I thought it was because you wanted me."

"I do, desperately," he said.

"You were so angry with me, Logan," she began.

"I know. I'm sorry." He drew her hand to his mouth. "I love Tansy, too, you see."

"I knew that. I was trying to protect you," she said miserably. "I thought if I waited, as Tansy wanted me to, until we knew the truth, it would be easier for you."

"You can't protect me from life," he said quietly. "I'm a grown man. I have the right to know what I'm up against. I've never run from anything."

"Except me," she murmured with an attempt at humor.

"You caught me, didn't you?" he mused.

"Well . . ."

"Tansy will be all right," he said. "She's sorry for what she thought, and I'm sorry for what I said. We'll both make it up to you somehow."

"There's no need for that."

"Yes, there is. Want me to tell you how I'm going to make it up to you?" he teased softly.

"No," she said, dropping her eyes to his chest. "You can wait . . . and show me."

He did. It took hours and hours, while he caressed her in the silence of their apartment, sprawled in loving abandon with her on the big king-size bed with all the lights blazing away.

He laughed at her shock, delighted in her hungry response, loved her from one side of the bed to the other and, finally, onto the floor with his inexhaustible ardor. It was dark before he was sated enough to rest.

They slept. When they awoke, he carried her into the bath and they lay together in the Jacuzzi, gently kissing, while they bathed. Afterward, they fixed steaks and salad in the kitchen and ate.

"Tansy was glad to see us," she said when she was curled up in his lap on the sofa, when they'd put the dishes into the dishwasher.

"And happy for us," he agreed. He bent and kissed her with soft possession. "I love you, Kit," he said huskily. It was evident in the eyes that swept over her, in the very softness of his voice. "I'll love you all my life."

"That goes double for me, Mr. Deverell," she murmured contentedly.

He leaned back with a long, happy sigh. "At least, we're free of Emmett," he said with a smile. "Tansy said he called and after the rodeo tonight, he'll be on his way to San Antonio with the kids."

"Who's keeping the kids?" Kit asked.

"A baby-sitter at the hotel." He chuckled. "I expect the poor woman will retire after tonight."

"No doubt." She linked her arms around his neck and lay her head on his broad chest. "I'm tired."

"So am I. And we both have a job to go to in the morning," he murmured. "I'm sorry I'm not a man of leisure. I'd like to stay in bed for several days."

"Me, too." She sighed. "But I guess life goes on."

"Thank God, it does." He tilted her face up to his and searched it hungrily. "I'm glad you didn't give up on me, Kit."

She smiled and drew his face down to hers. "How could I, when my life began the day I met you? Bad temper and all," she whispered against his hard mouth.

"I do *not* have a bad temper," he muttered.

"You do so!"

"I have never— What the hell are you doing?"

She pushed him down on the sofa and sat on him, laughing at his expression. "Showing you who's boss," she whispered. She laughed with aching delight as she eased down to his mouth and kissed him while her hands smoothed under his shirt. "Do you mind?"

"I don't know. That depends on whether you can make me like it," he whispered with ardent pleasure as her mouth settled on his. He chuckled as his hands went up to help her with his shirt. "So get busy. Show me!"

And several delightfully feverish minutes later, it was pretty evident that she'd done just that.

* * * * *

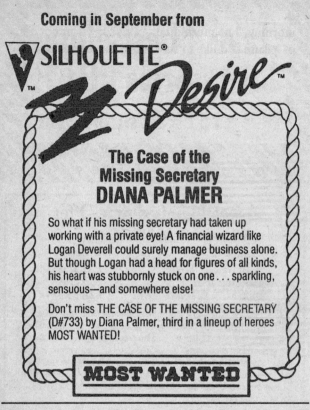

Take 4 bestselling love stories FREE

Plus get a FREE surprise gift!

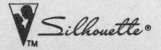

TAKE A WALK ON THE DARK SIDE OF LOVE

October is the shivery season, when chill winds blow and shadows walk the night. Come along with us into a haunting world where love and danger go hand in hand, where passions will thrill you and dangers will chill you. Come with us to

In this newest short story collection from Sihouette Books, three of your favorite authors tell tales just perfect for a spooky autumn night. Let Anne Stuart introduce you to "The Monster in the Closet," Helen R. Myers bewitch you with "Seawitch," and Heather Graham Pozzessere entice you with "Wilde Imaginings."

Silhouette Shadows™
Haunting a store near you this October.